Shattered Heart

A Novel

By Crystal Joy

Author of *Completely Captivated, Completely Yours,* and *Shackled Heart*

Edited by: Daisycakes Creative Services
Cover design by: Lyndsey Lewellen
Interior Design and Formatting by: BB eBooks

Print Edition
ISBN: 9781097170081

For Mandie: We met at just the right time, just the right place, to build a foundation of a beautiful friendship.

You are worthy of the sweetest love! ♡

XOXO,

Crystal Joy

Table of Contents

Chapter 1

AMANDA MEYERS BENT over the base of the bed, her gaze resting between her patient's spread legs. A dark head of hair blocked the birth canal. "I can see baby Emma."

Mac collapsed back onto a puffy pillow as she experienced another strong contraction. Screaming, she dug her fingernails into her husband's forearm. "I can't do this anymore."

"Yes, you can." Amanda sat up straighter and pushed back her shoulders, stretching out her muscles. A dull headache crept into her forehead, but she ignored it. After laboring for twelve hours, Mac needed Amanda's support now more than ever. "Are you ready to push again?"

Mac shook her head as a defeated look emerged in her heavily lidded eyes.

Amanda sent Mac an encouraging smile. Most of her patients at the Heartland Birth Center doubted their abilities at some point during labor, especially first-time moms like Mac. But the human body could perform miraculous feats. At the end, with their precious treasures cuddling on their chests, women often felt proud of how well their bodies had endured labor.

That was the best part about being a midwife—helping patients gain confidence in their physical abilities.

Mac leaned forward and expelled several quick breaths as another contraction started. "I want to push."

Amanda's chest swelled with pride. Mac was someone who had never wanted kids until she became an aunt. Seeing her transformation from no-way-I'll-never-be-a-mom to a waddling pregnant woman to now experiencing the last stage of labor was beautiful.

Mac's husband, Charlie, and one of the assistants grabbed Mac's bent legs.

"Whenever you're ready," said Amanda.

Mac let out a long, low grunt. Instead of moving, Emma's head stayed in the same position.

Amanda checked the fetal monitor. The heart rate had dropped from 130 to 120 beats per minute. Sudden drops in the heart rate weren't necessarily a cause for concern. Sometimes the umbilical cord could stretch and compress during labor, leading to a brief decrease in blood flow to the infant.

Charlie dabbed a wet washcloth on Mac's face and brushed her dark hair off her glistening forehead. "You're doing great."

A sense of longing tugged at Amanda's heart. Hopefully, this would be her and Tyler someday soon—married and having a little one of their own. After meeting at a holistic healthcare conference, they'd dated long-distance before Tyler Kelly had moved to Maple Valley to live closer to her. But after five years of dating, he still hadn't proposed. She'd given him subtle hints, watching *Say Yes to the Dress* and stopping in jewelry stores to *browse*. But something was holding him back.

Maybe he was waiting for this weekend.

She glanced up at the clock. Another midwife at the birth center was scheduled to take over for her in thirty minutes. Excitement bubbled in her chest. In just a few hours, she'd be on a plane with Tyler, replacing Iowa cornfields for Florida palm trees. They'd planned a short, relaxing trip for Labor Day weekend. And a great start to her vacation would be delivering Mac and Charlie's baby.

She checked the fetal monitor again. The heart rate had dropped to ninety beats per minute. Adrenaline coursed through her veins, fueling her with a sudden surge of anxiety. She asked Mac to change positions to see if it would make a difference.

It didn't.

Usually, she'd encourage her patients to listen to their bodies instead of telling them what to do, but

Emma might have stopped breathing. "There's no time to rest. Push."

Mac looked at Charlie and blinked back tears. She hunched forward, letting a loud scream escape through her clenched teeth.

Emma's head moved down a little farther but not much.

A knot formed in Amanda's stomach. If Mac couldn't push her daughter out soon, she would have to be rushed to Furnam Hospital thirty minutes away from Maple Valley. The birth center didn't have the tools or staff to perform a C-section. "You need to get Emma out now," she said in an urgent tone.

Mac beared down as tears streamed down her flushed face.

Emma's head slid out of the birth canal with the umbilical cord wrapped around her tiny neck.

Amanda's heart thudded hard and fast against her chest. Even though nuchal cords were fairly common, the appearance of a cord wrapped around a baby's neck heightened her blood pressure. Without wasting any time, she unwrapped the cord in one quick, fluid motion.

Mac pushed again. One of Emma's shoulders slid out, then the other shoulder.

Amanda held on to Emma as the rest of her little body appeared. She held her breath, waiting to hear

Emma's first, sweet cries, but the infant wasn't crying.

All of Amanda's muscles tensed at once. Blood pounded in her ears to the rhythmic racing of her heart.

The assistants in the room rushed into action. One of the assistants quickly cut the umbilical cord and took Emma from Amanda. The assistant suctioned Emma's mouth and nose, clearing out fluid before laying the baby on the bed next to Mac. Another assistant placed an oxygen mask over Emma's nose to help her breathe.

Amanda forced her gaze away from the baby and tuned out the frantic conversation around her. She needed to deliver the placenta and stitch Mac's tear. She worked on autopilot, still waiting for a sign that the baby was okay.

Finally, a faint cry filled the room.

The tension in Amanda's shoulders lifted slightly. At least Emma was breathing. But why wasn't her cry stronger?

The assistants worked on Emma for several more minutes before one of their voices rose above the others. "Emma's oxygen level is alarmingly low."

Amanda stopped stitching and looked up. "Then we need to fly Emma to the NICU at Furnam Hospital."

Mac's eyes widened, her expression panicked as she looked at Charlie, then Amanda. Her lips quivered. "Is Emma okay?"

Amanda gave Mac a weak smile. "Try not to worry.

Emma is in good hands." Even to her own ears, she knew her response sucked. But she wouldn't make promises she couldn't keep.

IN THE BIRTH center's locker room, Amanda shimmied out of her dirty scrubs into yoga pants and a T-shirt with her favorite quote scrolled across the front: *Be the energy you want to attract.* At the sink, she washed her face, then tossed her hair into a messy ponytail. For a brief moment, she considered putting on makeup, but after dating Tyler for five years, she felt comfortable not getting all dolled up for him.

And she didn't feel like it anyway. Not with the uncertainty of Emma's condition weighing on her mind.

Over the last few years, she'd seen and delivered multiple babies who needed to go to the NICU. Many babies had been born with nuchal cords, like Emma, and most often those babies were just fine. Some had swallowed meconium or too much amniotic fluid and needed a few hours to recover. Other infants had been born early and needed the extra care.

But she'd also seen rare cases when infants were born with life-threatening conditions. Hopefully, that wasn't the case for Emma and she wouldn't have to stay at the hospital for long.

Instinctively, Amanda clutched the locket at the base of her neck. She'd prefer not to remember the last time she'd visited Furnam Hospital.

Her phone vibrated on the counter. *Probably Tyler, wondering where I am.* He was supposed to pick her up and drive them to the airport. She glanced at her phone, seeing a message from Dad instead. *Have fun this weekend. Call me if you get something special.* Surprisingly, Mr. I-don't-understand-technology had added a winking emoji.

She rolled her eyes but smiled in spite of herself. So Dad wondered if this trip would end in an engagement, just like she did. Tyler had the whole trip planned—surfboard lessons at Cocoa Beach, a day at Epcot, and dinner reservations at the Rainforest Cafe. It would be the perfect trip for a proposal.

Slipping into a light jacket, she grabbed her duffel bag and walked quickly through the clinic. She dashed out into the night, scanning the brightly lit parking lot. Tyler's car wasn't here.

She chewed on her thumbnail. Tyler was never late. Usually, he liked to arrive early anywhere he went. Hopefully, nothing bad had happened, like a car accident or a … She stopped her thoughts from turning into worries. *Think positively.* Maybe a patient had shown up at Cory's Chiropractic, needing a last-minute adjustment. That seemed like a practical reason to be late. But even if that was the case, he could have at least texted her.

Amanda paced back and forth on the sidewalk. Her calves ached from Mac's long labor, but she couldn't sit still. If Tyler didn't get here soon, they would miss their flight.

A few minutes later, Tyler's Mercedes pulled into the parking lot at a leisurely pace and idled in front of the curb.

She flung open the passenger door. "Where—"

Tyler glanced in her direction and pointed to his cell phone. He lifted his pointer finger, signaling for her to wait.

Amanda tossed her duffel bag in the back and slid into the passenger seat. Who was he talking to? Based on his appearance, it didn't look like an easy conversation. His dark-blond hair looked slightly disheveled as if he'd been running his hands through it, and the sleeves of his dress shirt were haphazardly rolled up to his elbows.

Tyler spoke into the phone. "I'll be there tomorrow morning. Bye, Dad." He slipped his phone into the pocket of his dress pants and unbuttoned the top of his shirt, airing it out. "I have bad news."

"I take it we aren't going to Florida?"

"My dad needs me back in Chicago. Two of his chiropractors are sick with the flu. He's completely booked on Saturday, so he needs me to fill in. I'm so sorry."

Her dull headache turned into a throbbing pulse. She grabbed a bottle of peppermint oil from her purse and rubbed a little onto each of her temples as she contemplated what to say. "We've had this trip planned for months. You couldn't tell him 'no'?"

"I won't do that to my dad."

Amanda slumped back against her seat, fighting off disappointment, and losing the battle. "But you have no problem doing it to me." So much for being *the energy you want to attract*. But she couldn't help it. No romantic vacation. No secretly planned proposal. Her disappointment quickly escalated to frustration.

Tyler stared at the dashboard, his dark blue eyes unable to meet her gaze. He lowered his chin to his chest. "Honestly, I wasn't looking forward to this trip."

What? She froze for a moment, almost letting go of the bottle of peppermint oil as she waited for him to explain.

"Your dad left me a voicemail last night. He asked if I was going to propose to you on our trip."

"Seriously?" Leave it to Dad to meddle with her love life. Even though she was twenty-eight, he didn't know when to butt out. He'd done everything from reading her texts as a teenager, to following her on a first date, and now badgering her and Tyler about getting engaged.

"I didn't call him back. I didn't know what to say."

Tyler unrolled his sleeves to button the cuffs. "Everyone is always putting pressure on us to get married, especially your dad. And lately, you've been watching all those wedding dress shows and looking at rings …"

She frowned. So he had noticed after all.

"I wasn't planning on proposing during this trip, and after I heard your dad's voicemail, I figured you might have the same expectations. By the end of the weekend, you'd only be upset with me." Tyler ran a hand over his clean-shaven face. "I'm not ready to get married—you know what happened to my parents. They got married too quickly, hated each other for it, and then got divorced. I don't want that to be us."

His words knocked the wind out of her. How was she supposed to respond? Reassure him that it was okay? That her feelings weren't hurt? But none of that would be truthful. "It's not like we just met and we're rushing into an engagement."

He tugged at his tie and loosened the knot. Turning toward her, his lips formed a thin line and his Adam's apple bobbed up and down. "I think we should take a break."

She tightened her grip on the bottle of oil, then tossed it into her purse. No way had she heard him correctly. They were supposed to get married, start a family, and raise their kids in Maple Valley. Maybe not as quickly as she'd hoped, but she'd been willing to wait.

He reached for her hand, lacing his fingers between hers. "A break will give us time to think about what we want from this relationship."

"I already know what I want," she said quietly.

"I never intended to hurt you."

Amanda pulled her hand out of his grasp. "If you don't know what you want by now, then we aren't taking break." Anger slashed through the initial shock, shaking her to the core. "We're done."

She grabbed her duffel bag, flung open the door, and strode across the parking lot to her car without looking back. How could she have been so wrong about Tyler? He'd wanted a break when she'd been ready to commit to him forever.

TEN MINUTES LATER, Amanda drove along Ashmend Road, the steep, winding street stretching from downtown to the Wildwood Estates at the edge of Maple Valley. Normally, cars lined the side of the narrow road and pedestrians ambled across the street, waving at friends. But tonight, bright neon *Closed* signs hung in all of the shop windows.

Friday night football. Around here it was practically a sin not to go. Everyone went to the football games, unless they had a good reason, like Dad did tonight.

He'd been battling a cold and cough for the last few weeks. As a retired football coach, it was killing him not to be at the game, but she'd told him to stay home and rest. He was probably wrapped in a wool blanket on the couch, anxiously awaiting the news highlights.

She passed beneath the old, dim streetlights and lowered the windows. A light fall breeze drifted through her car. In the distance, the Mississippi River lapped against the shore. The only other sound came from her tires rumbling along the uneven brick road.

This was a first. She'd never been downtown during a football game. It was almost eerie, except it was more of a relief to be alone—so she didn't have to watch for sudden jaywalkers. She could barely focus on the road with Tyler's confession set on repeat. But no matter how many times she replayed the conversation, she came to the same conclusion. Tyler didn't want to marry her. Whether that meant right now or never didn't matter. She'd misread his feelings.

But how? Surely, when he'd moved to Iowa to be closer to her, he'd thought they might have a future. In the last few years, something must have changed his mind. He'd blamed it on her dad's pressure, but if he wanted to propose to her, it wouldn't feel like pressure, it would feel like reassurance. So many people, including Dad, supported their relationship.

She needed answers. Especially when she told Dad

the news. Part of her resented his nosiness, but Tyler's hesitancy was not Dad's fault. Her old man would be crushed when he heard about the breakup. His dreams of grandkids in the near future would crumble to dust.

Nearing the stop sign at the end of Ashmend Road, she pressed on the brakes. The streetlamp above her car flickered on and off, like a bad omen in a scary movie.

She shivered, contemplating where to go next. If she turned off the main road, she'd be home in a few minutes. She could hang out with Dad, but then she'd have to tell him the bad news, and she wasn't ready for that yet.

Maybe she should back up into the nearby alley and drive through downtown again. At least driving kept her mildly distracted from the unavoidable truth—she wasn't getting married to Tyler anytime soon. And after their conversation today, would she even take him back if he changed his mind? The angry part of her wanted to say no, but she *did* love him. He was smart, dependable, hardworking, and attractive. He had so many qualities that would make him a good husband.

The streetlamp turned black, leaving a portion of the road blanketed in darkness. She glanced at the rearview mirror, squinting. She couldn't see anything, but no one seemed to be around anyway. She shifted into reverse and backed up.

Something struck the back of her car. The sound of

crunching metal slashed through the silent night. She slammed on the brakes. Had she hit a dumpster or something?

Then, she heard a loud groan.

Her heart pounded hard against her chest. What if she'd hit a child? Or what if she'd run into Mr. Adams? His Alzheimer's was getting worse. Last week he'd wandered around Dill's Grocery until it closed and almost got locked inside.

She yanked open the door and rushed to the back of her car, halting in place. The streetlight flickered on, casting a dim glow on a motorcycle lying on its side. Several metal parts lay strewn across the road, dented at odd angles.

She scanned the area for the biker. A few feet away, a man was lying in the middle of the street. Her blood turned to ice. She ran closer and kneeled down beside him. "I'm so sorry. I didn't see you."

His eyelids fluttered open as he mumbled something incoherent.

A lump formed in her throat. The man wasn't wearing a helmet. "Did you hit your head?"

"No, I landed on my side," he answered in a husky voice. He flicked dark hair out of his face, exposing creamy chocolate eyes and long, dark eyelashes.

Amanda cupped a hand over her mouth. She'd hit Ethan Contos, the doctor from Greece. When Ethan had moved here a year and a half ago, he'd been the talk of the town. Heck, he still was. Her friends referred to him as the 'Greek god.' He acted like some hot commodity, dating most of the single women in Maple Valley.

Not that any of it mattered right now. She had to make sure Ethan was okay.

She ran her fingers along his neck and shoulders. Even if he hadn't hit his head, whiplash could still cause a concussion. "Do you feel dizzy or nauseous?"

"No."

"Do you have a headache?"

"No."

"Do you—"

"My head is fine," he snapped.

Amanda crossed her arms. Ethan was clearly in pain and had a right to be angry with her, but he didn't have to be rude. "You weren't wearing a helmet. I was just checking for a concussion, *Dr. Contos.*"

He squeezed his eyes shut, speaking quickly in what she assumed to be Greek. She had no idea what he was saying, but it sounded a lot like curse words.

Finally, he opened his eyes and met her gaze. "I usually wear my helmet, but I left in a hurry." His voice sounded strained as he shifted slightly and clutched his side. "Even doctors can be forgetful."

A pang of guilt coursed through her. She shouldn't have called him out like that. "What hurts?"

"My ribs." He pointed to his side.

She unzipped his leather jacket, exposing a white undershirt that clung to his well-defined chest. A thin slit cut through the side of his shirt.

She ran her fingers along his rib cage, feeling a small lump. Her mouth went dry. "It feels like you might have a broken or dislocated rib. It could be more than one rib, but I can't tell."

"Why didn't you see me? I was the only other person on the road."

"The streetlamp kept flickering on and off. When I backed up, it was too dark to see anything."

"You didn't see my headlight?"

"No."

Ethan slowly turned his head, looking at his motorcycle. "I can't believe this."

Amanda pursed her lips. He didn't have to interrogate her. She'd already apologized and taken blame. But then again, he hadn't been very coherent at first. Maybe he hadn't heard her apology. "It was an accident. I feel awful for hitting you."

He turned toward her, his eyes softening. "You're right. I'm not trying to make you feel bad. I'm just …" He sucked in a breath. "… in a lot of pain."

Her eyes widened, surprised by his admittance. "Do you want to get an X-ray? I can take you."

"Yeah." Grimacing, Ethan placed his hands behind

his back, attempting to sit. He could barely get his head off the ground.

"Wait for me to help you. I'll be right back. I need to make a quick phone call." Swallowing hard, she headed back to her car for her cell phone. The hospital was thirty minutes away. The closest place to get an X-ray was Cory's Chiropractic. It was the last place she wanted to go, but after damaging Ethan's motorcycle and injuring his ribs, it was the only peace offering she could think of.

If only helping him wouldn't break her heart in two.

Chapter 2

ETHAN CONTOS SHIFTED in the passenger seat, trying to ease the discomfort in his side. Instead, a sharp, needlelike pain sliced through his ribs.

At least when he arrived at the hospital, the doctor would give him pain meds. His body hadn't ached this much since he'd crashed Pappous' fishing boat into the dock and fell out, spraining his wrist.

But pain wasn't his biggest issue. The shock of the accident must have stunned his brain earlier, preventing him from thinking clearly. Now, reality hit him like a torrential downpour. If his ribs were broken, he wouldn't be able to carry out his responsibilities at the hospital. Most people with broken ribs were told to take it easy for four to eight weeks, but he only had four months of training left in the US—training that required him to be on his feet, taking care of patients in the oncology unit.

He clenched his fists. If he couldn't complete his training, his boss would probably tell him to go back to Greece early. As Americans said, that would be the worst-case scenario.

"I really am a good driver. I've never hit anything in my entire life." Amanda clutched the steering wheel and quickly glanced in his direction. Loose, blond curls had fallen out of her messy ponytail, framing her slender chin. "But maybe driving wasn't the best idea tonight."

"Why not?"

"I wasn't exactly focused on the road."

"You were distracted?"

She let out a long sigh. "Yeah."

His nostrils flared. He opened his mouth but closed it quickly, stopping himself before he could say something he regretted. He couldn't be mad at her. Not when he'd been distracted too. In hindsight, he should've played poker with some of his colleagues tonight, but after a phone call from his ex-wife, he'd decided to take a drive instead.

He'd needed an outlet to burn off steam. He hadn't spoken to Raechel since he'd moved to the US. Tonight she'd called to share her news—she was getting married to a widower with three kids. She'd wanted him to hear it from her before someone else called to tell him.

He scrubbed a hand over his face, immediately regretting his decision to move. Wincing, he clutched his side. He needed to keep the conversation going, so he wouldn't focus on his ex's news, or his ribs. "Why were you distracted?"

"I just broke up with my boyfriend."

"I thought you were getting engaged soon."

Her head swung in his direction, her eyes widening. "Who did you hear that from?"

"I hear a lot of rumors at Val's Diner from the old, purple hat ladies. Half the stuff they say are rumors, but I thought this one was actually true."

"I wish."

"Didn't you say you're the one who broke up with him?"

"Yes, but only because Tyler asked for a break."

"A break? As in, he wants to see other people?"

She lifted her chin, but her bottom lip quivered. "No, that's not it. Tyler would never do that."

"Sorry, that was uncalled for." Guilt settled in the pit of his gut. His ribs were throbbing, affecting his mood, but that wasn't a good excuse.

Amanda turned onto a side street, nearing the end of downtown.

His eyebrows furrowed together. "This isn't the way to the hospital."

"That's not where I'm taking you."

"Where are we going?"

"The hospital isn't the only place you can get an X-ray." She pulled into a small parking lot and stopped in front of Cory's Chiropractic.

Ethan's lips parted as he contemplated how to respond without being rude. He'd never gone to a chiropractor before and he didn't intend on going to one now. "Look, I'd appreciate it if you'd take me to Furnam Hospital."

"No way. I mean, I just don't feel comfortable there." She turned off the car, giving him her full attention. The lights from inside the building turned on, highlighting the reddish hue darkening her already-rosy cheeks. "You're in a lot of pain. This place is much closer than the hospital and they'll give you an X-ray for free."

"But if I have a broken rib, I'll need to see a doctor."

"And if you have a *dislocated* rib, Tyler can adjust you and fix the problem right away."

Ethan arched an eyebrow. "This wouldn't be the same Tyler you just broke up with, would it?"

"Yeah."

"Let me get this straight. You're taking me to see your ex?"

Nodding, she opened her door.

"You don't understand, I—" He didn't bother finishing his sentence. Amanda was already out of the car, rushing to the passenger side. Besides getting a free X-ray, this was a waste of time. No way would he let a chiropractor adjust him. He didn't mind if other people went to chiropractors to ease minor aches and pains, but after ten years of training and experience as an oncologist, Ethan only trusted doctors to fix his medical conditions.

Amanda opened his door, leaned over, and held out her hand. She gently pulled him to a standing position. He put his arm around her shoulders as she led him inside and stopped in the lobby. Without moving his arm, his face was inches away from hers.

He caught the faint scent of her flowery perfume, similar to the lilac bushes in his parents' backyard. The familiar scent made his chest tighten. His parents had barely spoken to him since his divorce. In their minds, he hadn't tried hard enough to make his marriage work.

But they didn't know all the details. No one knew why he and Raechel had divorced, and he planned to keep it that way. If his family discovered the truth, they might never speak to him again.

Footsteps approached from the hallway and stopped a few feet away.

Amanda fiddled with the zipper on her jacket as Tyler stepped into the lobby.

The knot of Tyler's tie hung loosely beneath the collar of his wrinkled button-down shirt. He immediately looked at Amanda, giving her an apologetic smile. His red-rimmed eyes filled with remorse and dark splotches appeared on his neck.

Ethan tilted his head slightly. Guys didn't look at their ex-girlfriends that way unless they wanted to get back together. He cleared his throat to ease the silent tension. These two had a lot of issues to work out.

Tyler focused his attention on Ethan. "Amanda told me your ribs might be broken or dislocated. What happened?"

"Amanda backed into my motorcycle and knocked me off."

Tyler stared at Amanda as if he couldn't decide if Ethan was telling the truth. "Are you serious?"

"No, Ethan's joking. I just wanted a reason to see you again." Sarcasm saturated her dry tone.

Whoa. Ethan bit back a grin. Amanda was a firecracker when she was angry. If he ever ran into her again, he'd have to remind himself to stay on her good side.

"I came here to help you, didn't I?" Tyler asked quietly.

"You're here to help *him*. He's in a lot of pain."

Tyler gave a slow nod before gesturing at Ethan to follow him. "Let's get an X-ray and see what's wrong."

Twenty minutes later, Ethan slowly lowered himself into one of the chairs in the exam room—or whatever chiros called the rooms where they gave adjustments. He tried to sit as still as possible, but every breath caused a sharp sting to slice through his side.

Amanda sat down next to him and patted his knee. "Is there anything I can do to make you feel better?"

He took a deep breath and let it out slowly. "Do you have any medicine in your purse?"

Amanda pulled a big purse into her lap, rummaging through the contents. "I have a bottle of lavender oil in here. It helps with pain relief."

"You don't have any aspirin or ibuprofen?"

"No, but lavender oil works just as well." Before he could respond, she lifted the bottle of lavender oil out of her purse and twisted off the cap.

A bead of sweat trickled down his back. This was ridiculous. First she took him to a chiropractor, and now she wanted him to use an essential oil. Frustration boiled within, but he wouldn't let Amanda know. She meant well.

She lifted up his shirt, her lips parting slightly. She dabbed the oil on her fingertip and brushed it over his ribs.

Her soft touch sent tingles down his spine, despite the pain emanating from his ribs. His gaze flickered down to her full and rosy lips. Before she noticed, he shifted in his chair and looked away. He clearly wasn't thinking straight. She'd just hit him with her car and had possibly broken his ribs. Maybe he *had* hit his head, after all.

"Lavender oil works quickly. You'll feel a difference soon."

"Oh." He didn't have the heart to argue with her. If she wanted to believe the oil would help him, then that was fine with him. "Where is Tyler?"

"I'm sure he'll back soon."

"I hope so. It's killing me."

Amanda's eyes filled with compassion and amusement. "You're being a little overdramatic, don't you think?"

"I don't mean physically." As the words left his mouth, he realized the pain had dulled a bit. Had the essential oil done something or was he just running on extra adrenaline? "I meant: it's killing me not to know if my ribs are broken."

"Oh."

"I'm here on a visa doing training, so if I can't work, I'll have to go back to Greece."

"You make it sound like you don't want to go home."

"I don't."

"Too busy enjoying all the women around here?" She cupped a hand over her mouth. "I, uh … I shouldn't have said that out loud. I mean, or at all."

Under different circumstances, she might have looked cute, all embarrassed. But what she'd said had stung. Was that what she thought of him?

Three knocks rapped on the door. Tyler stepped inside the room. Diverting his gaze away from Amanda, he eased down on a stool and turned toward the computer. "I have good news and bad news."

Ethan instinctively moved a hand over his ribs.

"What's the bad news?"

Tyler pulled up the X-ray and pointed to the computer screen, near Ethan's right side. "You have two dislocated ribs."

Ethan's shoulders loosened with relief. Recovering from dislocated ribs wouldn't be too bad. "What's the good news?"

"I can pop them back into place for you."

Amanda clasped her hands together. "That's great."

Great? Not exactly. Ethan shook his head, trying to keep his tone even. "I'd rather wait to see a doctor."

"My hips pop out of place a lot. I get adjusted once a month, and I always feel better after coming here," Amanda said.

"That's nice, but I don't want to get adjusted."

Amanda folded her arms over her chest. "Many of my patients even bring their babies in. It's safe."

"Patients?" He tried to remember what she did for a living, but he'd only seen her helping her dad at the Canine Palace.

"I'm a midwife at the Heartland Birth Center."

That explained a lot. The way Amanda had examined his head when she found him, the essential oil in her purse. No wonder she had dated Tyler. They probably had similar beliefs about holistic healthcare.

Tyler put his hands on his thighs, turning the stool away from the computer. "I won't force you to do anything you don't want to do, but I can adjust your ribs and spine. You might be sore afterward, but the pain you're feeling now ... It'll be gone."

Ethan didn't want to chance it. Tyler could mess up and make the dislocation worse.

And yet, without any medicine masking his pain, he still had a long night ahead. Amanda had to drive him home, his uncle would have to take him to the hospital thirty minutes away, and then he'd have to wait in the ER. The whole process would take at least a few hours.

Ethan cursed under his breath, hoping he wouldn't regret this later. "Okay. I'll try an adjustment."

Standing, Tyler ushered Ethan over to a body-length chair in the middle of the room.

Ethan lay facedown, staring out of a small, breathable hole as Tyler's thumbs moved up his spine. Every so often, Tyler would stop and press his palms into Ethan's back. Several cracks made a *pop, pop, pop* noise. Grunting, he felt his lungs constrict. *Those sounds better be normal.*

Five minutes later, Ethan stood and felt along his rib cage, then felt again, and again. The lump was gone. He could breathe normally. And not only that, but his side barely hurt. Smiling, he shook Tyler's hand. "Thank you."

"See?" Amanda grinned. "Aren't you glad you got adjusted?"

Ethan nodded to appease her. He wouldn't go that far, but he had to admit that the chiropractor had fixed his ribs. For that, he was grateful. He was even more grateful that he could stay in the US. The longer he stayed away from his family, the easier it was to keep the secret from them.

DID YOU HEAR about Raechel? Ethan read the text from his youngest sister, Sophia, and tossed his phone back on the nightstand. He rolled onto his back and squeezed his eyes shut, trying to block the early morning sunlight pouring through the bedroom window of his uncle's guesthouse.

Couldn't his sister have waited to text him? He almost laughed at the question. No, of course not. His ex-wife's short engagement would be the main topic of conversation in his family until she got married. He could already imagine his sisters getting together for brunch today, their eyes lighting with excitement, their hands moving wildly as they discussed Raechel's decision to marry someone ten years older.

A smile spread across his face. And he wasn't there to hear any of the gossip. He could ignore his sisters' phone calls and texts as long as he wanted. By the time he moved back, Raechel would be married and someone else's life choices would be more exciting to discuss.

Ethan opened his eyes and stretched. His smile faded as his muscles throbbed in protest.

His phone vibrated on the nightstand. He peeked at the caller—his oldest sister. Ignoring the call, he slowly moved out of bed and ambled toward the bathroom, feeling like an old man. If only he could lie on the couch and watch soccer all day, but he was supposed to take his cousins to an apple orchard later.

In the bathroom, he opened the cabinet and reached for a tube of Icy Hot. He rubbed the cream all over his back and shoulders, waiting for the gel to cool his tender muscles.

At least his ribs were better—thanks to Amanda and her ex. Ethan still couldn't believe they had broken up. Before last night, Ethan hadn't known her personally, but she seemed sweet, especially when she helped her dad at the Canine Palace, handing out free samples to people who were walking their dogs. Plus, she played a hand in everything that went on around here: volunteering at festivals, running health fair booths, or teaching yoga in the park.

From what he knew of her, he'd always thought Tyler was a lucky man, and meeting her last night only confirmed his assumptions.

And yet, Ethan couldn't blame Tyler for wanting to be single. His own life was much simpler without being tied down. In fact, lately he couldn't picture himself getting remarried, especially after talking to Raechel last night. She'd sounded excited to be getting married and to be a stepmom.

He was happy for her. But talking about kids with his ex-wife had resurrected all the broken dreams they'd shared and all the terrible fights leading up to their divorce. The more he thought about it, he couldn't think of one good reason to go through that kind of misery again.

Chapter 3

"THIS MIGHT BE a little cold." Amanda kneeled down beside the couch and tucked her chin to her chest as she rubbed gel on Kendall's baby bump. If she didn't make eye contact with Kendall or her husband, Zach, then they couldn't see Amanda's red-rimmed eyes.

Kendall sat up a little, pressing her elbows into the couch cushion. "No offense, honey, but you look awful. Are you sure you should be at work today? I can reschedule my appointment."

Amanda almost smiled. Only Kendall could make a brutally honest statement sound sweet at the same time. They'd been friends since elementary school. "I'd rather be here than sitting at home thinking about Tyler and wondering what went wrong."

Kendall pursed her lips. "I still can't believe he didn't tell you why he wanted a break."

Sitting at the end of the couch, Zach shook his head. "What a jerk."

Amanda nodded in agreement. And yet, she missed Tyler. Everything reminded her of him. The gluten-free crackers she kept in her purse because he liked to snack on them. The aroma of pumpkin lattes—his favorite drink in the fall. The extra pair of tennis shoes he'd left at her house in case they went for a run.

The part that hurt the most was wondering if they had a chance of getting back together. Going to Cory's Chiropractic had left her with more questions than answers. She still couldn't figure out why Tyler had looked so sad and acted so awkward. He was usually composed and confident. He must've been surprised that she'd broken up with him instead of agreeing to a break.

Unless Ethan was right, and Tyler wanted to see other women.

She frowned. But what would Ethan know? He didn't seem like the relationship type. He was every bit as stubborn as she'd expected from an arrogant ladies' man—initially questioning her for not seeing him on the road and stubbornly rejecting the possibility that a chiropractor could heal him.

At least he'd finally allowed Tyler to adjust him, so she had to give Ethan credit for that.

She lifted the fetal Doppler above Kendall's stomach and gently touched her friend's shoulder. "It'll be easier if you lie down all the way."

"Okay." Kendall bit down on her bottom lip. "I hate

this part."

"Why?" Frowning, Zach readjusted Kendall's legs on his lap. "This is my favorite part. We get to hear the baby's heartbeat."

"It's the waiting part that I hate." With her hands at her sides, Kendall clenched and unclenched her fists.

Amanda moved the fetal Doppler across Kendall's stomach, hearing static. "Sometimes it just takes awhile to find it." She pressed a little harder, moving the Doppler to the opposite side of Kendall's belly. Kendall was one of the happiest pregnant patients she'd ever had, but when Kendall came in for appointments, she grew tense. Before this pregnancy, Kendall had experienced three miscarriages, each one occurring in the first trimester. Thankfully, she was in her second trimester and the pregnancy was going well.

"Why haven't you found it yet?" Kendall's voice trembled.

Amanda moved the Doppler higher, catching a steady bum-bum-bum that came across the sound waves. She glanced at Kendall, then Zach, smiling. "One hundred and fifty four."

Kendall let out a relieved laugh. "What a little bugger."

"I think we have a stubborn one." Zach raised an eyebrow, a wry grin spreading across his face. "I wonder who he got that from?"

"You, of course." Kendall smiled.

Amanda wiped the gel off Kendall's stomach and helped her friend move to a sitting position. "Do you have any questions?"

"I do," Zach said.

Usually, most men stayed quiet during this part of the appointment, but not Zach. Could he catch the baby? Could he cut the umbilical cord? Kendall was lucky to have a husband like Zach, a man who was ready to settle down and start a family. "Any other questions?"

Kendall pulled her long maternity shirt down over her yoga pants. Now that she knew the baby was okay, she seemed like her happy, vivacious self. "You know what you should do? You should go out with someone else to make Tyler jealous."

"That's a terrible idea."

"Who's cute and single?" Kendall tapped a finger against her chin as if Amanda hadn't spoken. "Grant Paxton, Parker Woods, Ethan Contos—"

Amanda snorted.

"What? I listed some good options."

"Ethan is not a good choice."

"Just because he dates a lot doesn't mean he's a bad guy. You've never even talked to him."

"Oh, but I have. I didn't tell you everything that happened over the weekend." Amanda perched on the armrest of the couch, divulging the rest of the details from Friday night. She still felt awful for crashing into Ethan, but it was far more exciting to talk about him than Tyler.

"No way." Kendall's mouth hung open. Her voice rose louder as she spoke. "This is crazy. You break up with Tyler, then you spend the night with the Greek god."

Amanda scowled. "You make it sound much more scandalous than it actually was." But maybe Kendall had a point. If she dated someone else, it might make Tyler realize what he'd lost.

And yet, she shouldn't have to date someone else just for Tyler to come to his senses. He would have to do it on his own.

AMANDA SCANNED THE bleachers, waving at familiar faces dressed in black and orange. "Where do you want to sit?"

Dad stopped and clasped the metal handrail overlooking the football field below. Behind thick glasses, his eyes glistened with a faraway look. "Closest spot you can find." He gave her a sideways grin without looking away from the players on the field. "Nothing beats a Maple Valley football game on a Friday night."

Rolling her eyes, she squeezed next to the railing,

allowing more room for the crowd to move past them. It might take a few minutes before she could get Dad moving again. She'd tried to convince him to stay home, but he refused. He wouldn't miss two games in a row.

She watched him out of the corner of her eye. No doubt he was analyzing the football players as they warmed up on the field. Retiring from coaching hadn't erased his passion for the high school football team.

Not that she could blame him. Palpable excitement lingered in the air. Cheerleaders chanted, "We're back to attack; we'll show no slack," as they sent a girl twirling above their heads. A group of kids darted past her wearing painted paws on their cheeks. The student section roared to life as the first row of boys yanked off their T-shirts, exposing sloppily written T-I-G-E-R-S.

Dad was right. Nothing could beat a Maple Valley football game on a Friday night. Especially when all she wanted to do was forget *last* Friday night.

Like that was possible.

He pointed to a small opening in the stands. "Found a spot. Let's go before someone else takes it."

Amanda followed behind him. As they maneuvered through the crowd, several people called out to him, "Hey, Coach Meyers!"

Smiling, Dad waved back and unfolded his bleacher chair. "It's gonna be a good game. I can feel it." His smile quickly faded when he sneezed into his old, worn hanky. Wiping his nose, he crumpled the hanky and crammed it into his pocket, then started coughing again.

She rubbed his back until he stopped coughing. A month was far too long for a cold. She'd diffused essential oils in his bedroom, made green drinks, and cooked healthier meals for him, but his cold and cough were only getting worse.

Straightening, he grabbed a Kleenex out of his sweatshirt pocket and spit into the tissue, crumpling it quickly into the palm of his hand.

"Will you please make an appointment for an adjustment or acupuncture? Even a massage would help loosen all the crud stuck inside your chest." She waited for him to give his usual claim: *I'm fit as a fiddle.* But instead, he plopped down on his bleacher chair, not willing to meet her gaze. "Are you listening to me?" she asked.

"Sit down. You're blocking my view."

Amanda sighed. Dad was as stubborn as a mule. She knew better than to argue with him during a game. She'd let it go—for now. The football players lined up on the field, preparing for kickoff. All across the stadium, fans swung cowbells from side to side, screaming over the clattering noise.

She grabbed a cowbell out of her drawstring bag and joined the crowd. If only people would realize how beneficial holistic healthcare was for their bodies. She wondered if Ethan felt any different after getting adjusted. The look of relief on his face still brought a smile to her face. He *really* didn't want to move home yet. But who would want to stay in Iowa over Greece? It seemed odd. If she hadn't ridiculed him about his dating habits, maybe she would've thought to ask.

A whistle blew and the kicker for the Tigers sent the ball to the twenty-yard line. One of the Rowling High School Spartans caught the ball and sprinted toward the end zone. One of the Tigers tackled the Spartan to the ground.

In the first row, a little girl with pigtails stood on her mom's lap. She shot a small fist in the air. "Take that, Spartans!"

Dad nudged her with his elbow. "One day you and Tyler could have a little Tiger like her."

Amanda winced.

"Shoot, Minnow, I wasn't thinking." He sent her an apologetic look.

"It's okay." She couldn't be mad at him. He had said stuff like that so often, she wasn't surprised he'd slipped. Plus, her childhood nickname always made her smile. He had called her Minnow for as long as she could remember. Growing up, she'd been much smaller than her twin brother. Even now, she stood a full foot shorter than Caleb.

"I still don't get it." Staring at the field, Dad ran a

hand over his beard. “You’re a great catch. What does Tyler need to think about?”

She shrugged.

Dad squared his shoulders and puffed out his chest. “Do you want me to invite him over? I bet I can get an explanation out of him.”

“No way. I know exactly what you have in mind. You’ll try to talk to him while you clean your hunting rifle.”

“That’s a great idea.”

“Oh please. That’s what you were planning to do, isn’t it?”

“Possibly …” A slow smile crept across his weathered face. “I have a better idea. What if I asked Tyler to go hunting with Charlie and me?”

“Absolutely not.” She held up her palm for emphasis. “And since when does your business partner hunt?”

“He doesn’t yet. Before his baby was born, we were looking over the books for the Canine Palace and we started talking about hunting. Charlie seemed interested, so I asked him to go.”

“With Emma in the hospital, I don’t think it’s happening anytime soon.”

“Poor kid. I never knew a baby could have emphysema.”

“Me neither. I’ve never heard of Congenital Lobar Emphysema. When I called Mac yesterday she said that someone has a better chance of getting struck by lightning than having it." Amanda shifted on the cold bleacher. Her bad week paled in comparison to Mac and Charlie's. After doctors ran multiple tests on Emma and found no answers, they decided to do a CT scan on her. The scan showed one of the lobes in Emma's lungs expanding like a balloon and pushing into her other lobes and her heart. A surgeon needed to remove the lobe. Amanda couldn't imagine how scared Mac and Charlie were.

"I plan on visiting them tomorrow after Emma's surgery. Do you want to come with me?"

"I don't think that's a good idea. You're sick, so you shouldn't be around Emma."

"Oh, that's true. Well, you could go, then."

A lump formed in Amanda's throat. "I, uh, I think we should just send flowers. I have a busy day tomorrow."

Dad opened his mouth and closed it as if he wanted to say more. Even though she'd never told him that she didn't want to go back to the hospital, he would understand why it would be hard for her to go. "Even if Charlie can't go hunting for a while, I could still ask Tyler to go with me. It would be good for him. I think that city-boy just needs a reminder that your old man has a gun."

Smirking, she shook her head. "You wouldn't hurt a

fly."

"Tyler doesn't need to know that." Dad's smirk disappeared, his face growing serious. "Honestly, if you want my real opinion ... Tyler wasn't right for you anyway."

The crowd roared and got to their feet as the Tiger quarterback ran into the end zone for a touchdown. Dad jumped up with them, putting two fingers in his mouth and whistling.

Amanda stood with the crowd and rang her cowbell, but her mind couldn't focus on the game any longer. She gently squeezed Dad's arm to get his attention. "I thought you liked Tyler."

"I do. He's always treated you right, until that stupid suggestion for a break, anyway. And he seemed to make you happy, but ..."

"But what?"

"You never had a spark in your eyes when you were around him. When your mom and I dated we couldn't get enough of each other."

She dropped the cowbell on her tennis shoe. The weight of the bell sunk into the top of her shoe and struck her foot. "Ouch!" Plopping down on the metal stand, she lifted her foot and clutched her shoe.

"Are you okay?" Dad lowered into his bleacher chair, giving her his full attention.

"Yeah, I was just surprised you brought up Mom."

Ever since Mom died, he rarely talked about her. But she knew how much Dad missed her. Amanda had caught him watching old recorded videos or staring at Mom's picture above the mantel on numerous occasions.

In those moments, she hoped Dad remembered Mom's better days. Amanda's own memories were tainted with Mom's final years as she grew worse and worse, until the day she was gone.

After Mom died, Amanda made a vow to herself to take care of Dad. Maybe if she'd taken better care of Mom, she would still be alive.

Dad coughed again. He covered his mouth with a Kleenex and a dark red color seeped through the thin tissue.

Her eyes widened and a sinking feeling settled in the pit of her gut. She put her hand over his before he could hide the tissue in his pocket again. "Is that blood?"

"GOOD MORNING." ETHAN stopped at the side of his patient's bed and pressed a button to move her into an upright position.

Lydia Evans turned her gaze away from *The Price is Right*. Her toffee-colored features looked paler than normal and her cheeks more sunken-in than they had been during her first round of chemo.

"How would you rate your pain today?"

Lydia squeezed her eyes shut, opened them, and sent him a forced smile that disappeared all too quickly. "About a six."

"You don't have to act so strong, you know."

"Oh, but I do." She glanced at the picture frames on the end table. In one photo, her teenage twins stood side by side dressed in their Sunday best, and in the other frame was a picture of Lydia and her husband kissing on a beach.

Ethan pressed the stethoscope above Lydia's heart. Hearing a strong, steady beat, he moved his stethoscope to examine her lungs. "Promise me if you're in a lot of pain, you'll let me or one of your nurses know, so we can increase your meds."

Lydia held up her hand, sticking out her pinky finger. "I pinky promise."

Ethan stared at her finger for a moment. "What's a pinky promise?"

She laughed. "You don't do pinky promises in Greece?"

"Nope. You'll have to fill me in."

As she explained, he looked down at the floor, then forced himself to meet Lydia's gaze. Sometimes, it was hard to look her in the eyes. How did she stay so positive? She had stage three lung cancer. Her prognosis wasn't good, but he and his team would do everything they could to prolong her life.

He reached for her arm and pressed two fingers on her wrist to check her pulse. "Your heart and lungs sound good. Your pulse is a little fast, but not too concerning."

Lydia nodded.

"Have you had any nausea?"

"No, thankfully. Molly and Mick baked me an apple pie that I can't wait to eat."

Ethan licked his lips. "Your kids are amazing." An unexpected ache crept into his chest. Years ago, he'd imagined having kids of his own—four or five at least. Now that dream seemed as far-fetched as winning a Nobel Prize.

Lydia lifted her chin. "Molly got first place at our county fair three years in a row."

Ethan whistled, trying to keep the conversation light. "How come she hasn't brought me any pie? I'd like to judge it for myself."

"I'll tell you what: if I go into remission again, she'll bake you a whole pie."

His chest constricted. Would Lydia go into remission again? It was a long shot, but it was possible. He'd witnessed miracles before, starting with his youngest sister.

But sometimes cancer struck twice. Lydia was a prime example. She'd been breast cancer free for ten years. Now it was in her lungs and back with a vengeance.

It was his turn to plaster a smile on his face. "Your nurse will be back in to check on you." He left the room and walked out into the hallway, pulling out his cell phone. More texts from his sisters about Raechel, all of which he refused to answer. He checked his work inbox for new emails. On busy days, it was the only way he could keep up with responses.

One of the subject lines read: *Ray Meyers.* His eyebrows furrowed together at the familiar name. He opened the email, clicked on Mr. Meyers' file, and scrolled through the content. His thumb paused above the address. Ray Meyers lived in Maple Valley. It had to be Amanda's dad.

He scratched at his jaw, conflicted. He had an excuse to see Amanda again.

Not that anything would ever happen between them, but he had to admit he'd thought about her more than he expected. The night they'd met, she'd dislocated his ribs, but the experience with her was so different from the last time he'd injured himself in Greece. He'd sprained his wrist and Raechel had driven him to the ER. It was a fairly simple process, but it had been hell. They'd argued the entire time, and he'd finished the night with a headache to go along with his sprained wrist.

Amanda was different. She'd kept a steady stream of

conversation to distract him from the pain. Well, that part made sense. After all, she helped women through labor on a regular basis. Dealing with a cranky stranger must have been child's play.

And that wasn't all. It was the way she'd tenderly touched his side; the way her big, blue eyes had filled with concern when he'd clutched his ribs; the wide smile that had spread across her face after his adjustment, as if she'd shared a portion of his pain.

But now she'd be the one in pain. The kind of pain that scratched at your insides until you felt raw. He knew the feeling all too well. It never went away completely. The fear of losing someone you loved and knowing you couldn't do anything about it.

He squeezed the back of his neck. Amanda's life was about to change forever. And he would be the one to deliver the devastating news.

Chapter 4

AMANDA TURNED OFF the ignition with trembling fingers. She peered through the windshield, staring up at the recently renovated Furnam Hospital. The circular gray building towered above the parking lot with twelve floors of windows overlooking a well-manicured lawn.

Her stomach churned as if she'd swallowed a stick of butter. Ten years ago, she'd rushed through those heavy glass doors with her twin brother. A nurse had called, advising them to come soon. *Your mom doesn't have much time left.*

Amanda dropped her head against the steering wheel and squeezed her eyes shut, trying to push away the memories. If only Caleb were here now. But he'd enlisted in the air force as soon as they graduated from high school, right after his girlfriend—and Amanda's best friend—had moved away.

Moisture built beneath her eyelids. Caleb didn't know that Dad might have cancer. *No use worrying your brother while he's off fighting in Iraq,* Dad had said. *I'll call him after I get my biopsy results.*

Dad had waited to tell her too, but after she'd seen the blood, he'd told her everything. He'd been spitting up blood for several weeks. Concerned, he'd gone to their family doctor, then he'd had a CT scan, an ultrasound, and most recently, a biopsy.

Amanda straightened and opened her eyes, blinking rapidly. She'd wanted to avoid this place for the rest of her life, but now she couldn't. She needed to be here for Dad. He had an appointment in fifteen minutes to find out the results of his biopsy. He was probably inside already, waiting for her to arrive. She'd driven separately so she could do a home visit with one of her pregnant patients who lived close to the hospital.

A bad idea. A million questions had prevented her from focusing on her patient. Did Dad have cancer? If he did, how bad was it? What were the chances of his survival?

If she didn't go inside the hospital, she'd miss his appointment and the opportunity to ask those questions. Channeling all of her willpower, she got out of her car and walked inside.

In the lobby, the sun shone through the large windows, reflecting off expensive-looking artwork hanging from the vaulted ceiling. Metal statues of horses stood in the middle of the space. Colorful lights blinked above the elevator doors.

She resisted the urge to shake her head. Too much money had been spent to renovate this place. It looked like some high-tech futuristic building. Just stepping inside made her feel cold, which was exactly how she *didn't* want her patients to feel. The birth center employees prided themselves on creating a warm, comfortable environment for moms and their families, a home away from home.

A loud ding echoed through the large space as the elevator doors opened. Amanda hurried toward the open doors, then stopped mid-step.

A woman inside the elevator stuck out her arm, preventing the doors from closing. "Are you going up?"

Amanda stared at the woman but couldn't speak. The last time she'd set foot in this elevator, she'd been leaving the hospital. Leaving Mom after saying their final good-byes.

"Are you coming?" the woman asked.

A lump the size of a golf ball formed in her throat. Heat radiated through her body. She fanned her face, trying to cool down. It didn't work.

"Amanda," said a familiar voice across the lobby.

She turned, her heart hammering hard and fast against her chest. White spots clouded her vision, making the lobby blurry.

A man raced toward her. "Amanda!"

Ethan? Before she could be certain, her knees buckled and a dark fog pulled her under.

AMANDA BLINKED REPEATEDLY as she regained consciousness. The bright fluorescent lights on the ceiling stung her eyes. Every muscle in her body tensed at once when she realized she was on the floor.

She opened her eyes fully and peered up at Ethan as he leaned over, cupping her head in his lap. Dark, thick hair fell across his forehead. He sent her a lopsided grin, making the cleft in his chin more pronounced. "We have to stop meeting under these kinds of conditions."

"What happened?" she mumbled.

He swept loose curls out of her face and tucked them behind her ear. "I was on my way to your dad's appointment when I saw you standing in the lobby. I waved at you, but you just stared at me for a minute, then fainted."

She rubbed her head, expecting to feel tender from where she'd landed, but her head felt fine. "Did you catch me?"

His cheeks turned red. "Uh, no. I didn't get to you in time. Thankfully, your body slowly crumpled to the floor and you didn't land hard."

"Oh." Relieved, she sat up quickly. The movement

caused a wave of nausea to course through her body.

"Whoa, just rest for a sec." Ethan kept his hand on her back, concern etched across his dark features. "Give yourself a chance to recover."

"I don't have time. I need to get to ..." She let the sentence trail off as his explanation finally sunk in. Ethan had been on his way to Dad's appointment. "You're the oncologist we're meeting with."

He tilted his head and shrugged with one shoulder. A gesture that did nothing to ease the fear camped out in her heart.

Ten minutes later, Amanda walked into Ethan's office. She lifted her chin and pushed back her shoulders. She had to act strong. No way would she tell Dad that she'd fainted. Minutes ago, she'd been certain she could pull it off. Mostly because of Ethan. On their way to the oncology floor, he'd asked several questions about Dad and his time as the Maple Valley football coach. She'd known exactly what Ethan was doing, purposely keeping her distracted and calm, but she'd answered all his questions anyway, feeling a bit better.

Until now.

Dad sat on the edge of his chair, gripping both armrests. He turned in her direction, his face as white as his beard.

She pressed a hand against her chest. He'd been sitting alone in this much-too-modern office, anxiously waiting to hear his test results. She should've tried harder to calm down before she got worked up, before she'd had a panic attack. It was *his* health in jeopardy, not hers.

Amanda rushed across the room and sat down in the chair beside him. "Sorry I'm late."

"It's okay." Dad gave her a shaky smile that disappeared so quickly she wondered if she'd imagined it.

"It's a pleasure to meet you, Mr. Meyers." Ethan extended his arm and shook hands with Dad. "I'm Dr. Contos, one of the thoracic oncologists at Furnam Hospital."

"You can call me Ray."

Ethan nodded. "Amanda told me that you're a football legend. I hear you took the Tigers to the state championship three years in a row."

Dad scratched the back of his head. "Am I missing something? Have you two met before?"

She sent Ethan a panicked look, silently pleading, *Please don't say anything about fainting or the car accident.* It was embarrassing to think she'd hit the only other person on the road. And she didn't want Dad to know that she'd called Tyler asking for a free adjustment. Even though she'd had good intentions, it seemed lame. She'd contacted Tyler thirty minutes after their breakup. How pathetic.

Ethan sat down behind a mahogany desk, then turned to Amanda, his gaze lingering a bit longer. "We, uh … we ran into each other a couple of weeks ago during a football game."

"Oh." Dad looked from her to Ethan as if he didn't believe the explanation, or maybe he didn't care. No doubt he had much more serious matters on his mind.

Ethan restacked a few pamphlets on his desk, his expression turning somber. "Mr. Meyers … Ray …"

She squeezed Dad's hand three times—their silent way of saying *I love you*. Hopefully, he didn't notice that her hand was trembling.

"There is a cancerous tumor in your lungs." Ethan delivered the news like a meteorologist stating the forecast. "You have non-small cell lung carcinoma, or in other words, stage two lung cancer."

Dad stared at Ethan for a moment, then slumped back against his chair.

Amanda shook her head as if she could shake away the diagnosis. She wanted to scream at Ethan and tell him that he was wrong. Dad just had a bad cold. He would feel better soon and their lives would return to normal.

She knew she was lying to herself, trying to cope, but right now, she didn't have the will to let reality sink in.

Ethan leaned forward, resting his elbows on his desk. "It's non-small cell lung cancer, which is considered a localized cancer. The tumor is larger than stage one tumors and the cancer has begun to spread to nearby lymph nodes. But the good news is it hasn't spread to distant organs."

Dad's Adam's apple bobbed up and down. "Can I see the biopsy results?"

Ethan gave a curt nod, his face unchanging as he turned the computer screen, showing an image of the tumor. He probably heard the same responses day after day, but she wanted to reach across the desk, grab him by the shoulders, and tell him this time was different. This time it was *her* dad and he didn't deserve to have cancer. He'd already been through enough when he lost Mom.

Ethan's eyes filled with compassion. "I know this news comes as a shock."

Amanda frowned. Ethan sounded genuine, but he didn't understand. He was just a knowledgeable messenger who had a fancy degree. What did he know about watching a loved one suffer?

"We've seen this before and seen people beat it. It's going to be a hard fight, but you can do it."

"How long do I have to live?" Dad croaked.

"A five-year survival rate for this type of cancer is thirty percent." Ethan picked up one of the pamphlets and held it up so they could see. The cover showed two images—a lung before surgery and a lung after. "First, I'd suggest surgery to remove the tumor."

"Will surgery remove all of the cancer?" Amanda asked quietly.

"Not necessarily. There might be a risk that cancer cells will be left behind during surgery. If that's the case, I'll recommend treatment."

Dad cleared this throat. "What kind of treatment?"

"Chemotherapy or radiation, most likely. I'll speak with your surgeon before we make any decisions."

Dad grabbed a Kleenex off the desk and coughed into it, spitting up blood. He didn't bother to hide the red-stained tissue from her this time.

She stared at the blood. Heat burned beneath her eyes and cheeks. Dad really had cancer. One of the leading causes of death in the United States.

Seconds passed when no one spoke. The clock on the wall gave a quiet *tick, tick, tick*.

Instinctively, she moved her hand toward her necklace and clasped the gold locket. It wasn't just death that scared her. Dad's body might wither away, his physical health deteriorating until he didn't have the will to live anymore. Just like Mom.

THE NEXT MORNING, Amanda flung a pink scarf over her long-sleeved pajama shirt and stepped out onto the deck in her slippers. A dense fog lurked above the Mississippi River and early morning sunlight peeked above the tall pine trees surrounding their land.

She sunk into the swing next to Dad and handed him a mug.

"Please tell me that's coffee." His voice sounded hoarse, probably from the incessant coughing she'd heard last night.

"No, it's tea with honey and lemon mixed in it. You need nutrients in your body, not caffeine."

He nodded and took a sip of his tea.

Amanda leaned her head on his shoulder. It still didn't seem possible that he had cancer. He was her rock. The man who woke her up early on weekends just to see the sun rise; who wrote quotes about life on sticky notes and left them on the kitchen table for her; who had taught her never to give up no matter how difficult the circumstances.

She chewed on the inside of her cheek, biting back emotions. "Have you talked to Caleb yet?"

"I called him last night. He offered to come home to visit, but I told him not to." Dad wrapped his fingers around the mug. "Maybe surgery will be enough to get rid of the cancer and we can put all of this behind us."

Was that what he actually believed or was he just saying that to make her feel better? "But what if they don't get all the cancer cells out? Will you do treatment?"

Dad readjusted the wool blanket draped across his lap and looked out at the river. "I don't know yet." His voice hitched, sounding like a hiccup. "If treatment could give me five more years, then it might be worth it. A lot could happen in that time. Caleb might move back. You might get married and start a family." Behind thick lenses, his eyes glistened. "You know how much I want to be a grandpa."

Her throat thickened. "But what if ...?" She let the sentence trail off, trying to stay composed. "Chemo is an invasive treatment. There are a lot of bad side effects that could harm you. If that's the case, would it be worth it?"

He patted her knee. "That's the million dollar question, Minnow."

Amanda snuggled closer to him, inhaling a mixture of peppermint and Old Spice cologne. There had to be another way—an option that could heal Dad, but not hinder his immune system.

She refused to let him suffer, like Mom had. Mom had taken a lot of different medications that were supposed to help her. Instead, she'd gained thirty pounds, losing what little confidence she had left; she'd been so tired that she'd stayed in bed and slept most of the day; and she'd developed hyponatremia, which had caused dangerous amounts of fluid to build up in her cells—all side effects of her medications.

If the pills had worked, the side effects would have been worth it. But no medications had saved Mom's life in the end.

Amanda straightened. Later today, she would scour

the internet to find a better treatment option for Dad. She was determined to find a different option, one that Ethan, or any other oncologist, probably wouldn't agree with.

Chapter 5

ETHAN STRADDLED HIS motorcycle and slipped on leather gloves. Sunlight poured through the open garage door, warming his face. It was a shame to wear a helmet on such a warm fall day, but no way would he make that mistake again. Especially not on his first ride since the accident.

He turned the ignition and the bike purred to life, rumbling beneath his thighs. The motorcycle was as good as new. Amanda had referred him to Jerry's Cycle Shop and paid the entire bill. He almost smiled, but thinking of Amanda made his stomach coil. She'd been a wreck at the hospital. It had been a week since then, and he'd thought about her every day. How she'd squeezed her dad's hand to support him. How her body had gone rigid with shock when she'd heard the diagnosis. How her rosy cheeks had paled and her big, blue eyes had filled with grief as she began to accept the horrible truth. All the while, he had to resist the urge to wrap his arms around her.

Meeting with new patients and telling them they had cancer was one of the worst parts about being an oncologist. Many people cried and the look of despair on their downcast faces remained etched into Ethan's memory.

But he would do everything he could to save Ray Meyers' life. At least Amanda was also in the medical field. Supportive family members were always great assets to patients. He wondered if Ray had any other family who lived in Maple Valley.

He reached for his helmet as a familiar red Ford Escort pulled into the driveway, parking a few feet away.

He arched an eyebrow as Amanda stepped out of her car, wearing sweatpants and a gray sweatshirt. Big, round sunglasses covered her eyes and her lips were parted slightly, making it impossible to read her expression.

As she walked closer, he noticed how the sun highlighted the light hues in her blond hair and browned the freckles speckled across her nose.

"I was just thinking about you." He wanted to take back the words the moment they left his mouth. *Real smooth.* "What I meant was … I was thinking about your dad. I hope his surgery goes well tomorrow."

She stopped in front of him, folding her arms over her chest. "That's what I need to talk to you about."

"Okay." He turned off his bike and waited for her to speak.

"What's the likelihood that you'll recommend chemotherapy or radiation?"

"Every patient is different, but typically treatment after surgery is beneficial just to make sure the cancer cells are gone."

Amanda licked her lips. "What if my dad only uses alternative medicine and natural approaches?"

Ethan stared at her for a moment. Was she serious? Judging from the things she'd said at Cory's Chiropractic, she probably was.

His gut hardened. He rolled his shoulders and neck, contemplating how to respond. "Look, if natural approaches saved that many lives, I would change my profession right now."

She removed her sunglasses, revealing a firm and somber expression. "Invasive treatments are toxic. You're not putting that poison in my dad."

"It does hinder the immune system, but it also kills cancerous cells."

"Hinder? You must be joking. It affects your digestive system, hair, nails, skin, and blood." She moved her hands wildly as she spoke, reminding him of his sisters. "It could cause permanent damage to your brain, liver, hearing …" She stopped speaking as her bottom lip quivered.

Ethan moved off his bike in one swift motion and set his hands on her shoulders. "It's okay. That's why I'm training in the US. I'm learning a procedure for stimulating the immune system during chemotherapy. If your dad needs chemo, then I'll also recommend immunotherapy."

"Let me guess: immunotherapy also has serious risks."

He ran his tongue over his teeth. "Of course it does, but it has proved to be very effective so far."

Amanda shook her head. "I'm sure you'll never understand what I'm about to say." She reached for her necklace, clutching the locket near her collarbone. "If my dad doesn't make a decision on his own and he asks for your opinion, please don't convince him to do invasive treatment."

What? He wanted to tell her that she was out of line, that her request was impossible, but the way she was looking at him—like he held the key to her happiness—prevented him from saying so. "If your dad asks for my opinion, I have to be honest with him. But I won't force him to do anything he doesn't want to do."

She slowly nodded and slid her sunglasses back over her eyes. "There's nothing I can say to make you change your mind?"

He let out a deep, weighted sigh. "No. Not when your dad's life is at stake."

RAY MEYERS KICKED the white linen sheets to the end of the ICU bed. Now that the anesthesia had worn off, he felt restless. At least that damn tumor was out of his body. He didn't want some foreign monster living inside of him.

This wasn't supposed to happen. He'd quit smoking years ago. He still remembered the day he'd decided to quit. A speaker had visited Amanda and Caleb's class. The woman had showed a video of an old man talking with a tube connected to the hole in his throat. After school, Amanda and Caleb had run to the football field and begged him to stop. He'd squatted in front of them and kissed their foreheads. *I'll do anything for my dynamic duo.* And he had—it had taken a few months, but eventually, he'd stopped.

Anger boiled from the deepest recesses of his soul. It didn't seem fair. Most of his life, he'd been a healthy guy. A little overweight, but he'd eaten fruits and vegetables every day. He'd exercised five times a week. Why had this happened to him? To his family?

Before he could think about it for too long, he tried to change positions. He pressed his palms into the hard mattress, but he couldn't move much. A blood pressure cuff was attached to his arm and an important-looking tube was coming out of his chest, attached to a canister where fluid drained out.

He turned his head and searched for the TV remote.

It was probably on the side table, but he couldn't see it. The small table was cluttered with a breathing tool—some silly contraption he had to use to practice taking breaths in and out—and several flower arrangements.

One vase held tulips with a dog-themed balloon tied to it. Those had to be from his partner at the Canine Palace. Charlie and Mac were staying at the hospital while Emma recovered. Thankfully, her surgery had been successful and she'd be able to go home soon. Her doctors said she'd grow up like any other kid and be able to participate in any physical activities she wanted to.

Ray's chest tightened. He could only hope for similar successful results.

He shifted slightly onto his side. He reached for the table, digging between flower arrangements. The remote had to be in there somewhere.

Dr. Contos knocked on the door, his voice rising as he strode across the room. "What are you doing, Ray? You could rip your chest tube out."

"I'm gonna go crazy if I have to lie still all day."

"You shouldn't move until a PT helps you. Someone will be in to see you later today." He pointed to buttons on the rail attached to the bed. "In the meantime, you can use these to turn on the TV, channel surf, and change the volume."

"Oh." Ray turned away from the table, wincing as the incision flamed beneath his hospital gown.

Dr. Contos pulled the sheets back over Ray's lap, his expression softening. "Were you awake when your surgeon came in to talk to you?"

"Yuppers." His voice shook and his hands suddenly felt clammy. "Sounds like the surgery was good."

The oncologist nodded, but his lips formed a thin line. "There's still a risk that cancer cells could be present, though."

Ray collapsed back onto his pillows, defeat flushing through his body in a wave of heat. *No, no, no.*

Dr. Contos sat down on the edge of the bed. He looked over his shoulder as if he expected someone else to enter and waited a few seconds before turning back to Ray. "Are you open to doing treatment? If so, I would recommend chemotherapy."

Ray glanced out the large window on the far side of his room, replaying his latest conversation with Amanda. *Our bodies are amazingly designed to fight invaders,* she'd told him. She'd found several studies about cancer patients who had only used holistic approaches to curing cancer and succeeded. The patients had changed their lifestyles by eating better; using essential oils; and doing alternative therapies, like acupuncture, massages, homeopathy, and naturopathy—whatever the heck that was.

And Amanda wholeheartedly believed that he could have the same outcome. But he wasn't so sure. "I need more time to think about it."

"I understand." Dr. Contos rested his hands on his thighs and his eyes filled with concern. "Just so you know, the sooner you start chemo, the better your chances are of it working."

A sheen of sweat trickled down his forehead. Amanda and Caleb didn't deserve to see another parent die, not like this. He wasn't going down without a fight. At sixty-eight, he still had a lot of living left to do. But would his fight include chemo or not?

Dr. Contos shifted on the bed. "Do you have any big plans for the next ten years?"

"When I retire, I'd like to go on a fishing trip somewhere far away from Iowa."

The doctor smiled. "So you're a fisherman."

Ray nodded. "I have a cabin right off the Mississippi. It's a great spot for catching big mouth bass."

"I love to fish. My family owns a fishing company in Greece."

A guy who likes to fish? A lot of boys in Maple Valley grew up fishing, but none of them made time for it anymore. Even his old buddies preferred to stay off the water nowadays, playing poker at Val's Diner instead of spending a day on the river. It was a shame. "Fishing in the Mediterranean—now that's something I've never done. What do you usually catch?"

"Mackerel, squid, octopus, cuttlefish, and lobster."

"What's the biggest fish you've ever caught?"

The oncologist pushed his shoulders back, his smile widening. "When I was a teenager, my dad and I caught a five-meter shark. It weighed over 300 kilos. We'd never seen anything like it."

Ray whistled. "That must've been something."

"That one fought us real hard. We had to let it go, though."

"Did you get a picture of it?"

Dr. Contos nodded. "Oh yeah. It's very rare to see sharks in those waters. We wanted a picture for bragging rights."

Ray laughed, the foreign sound surprising him. Between his diagnosis and Amanda's breakup, he'd had very little to laugh about lately. It tore his heart to hear Amanda crying in her room. The paternal, protective part of him wanted to storm inside Cory's Chiropractic and demand that Tyler give Amanda answers. But Amanda had made it quite clear: she wanted him to butt out.

"Where can I get a decent rod and reel?" the doctor asked.

"Dill's Grocery in Maple Valley has a small bait shop next to it. Or you could borrow one of mine and we could go out on my boat sometime."

"That would be great."

Ray smiled. Finally something he could look forward

to. Dr. Contos seemed like a good guy.

Standing, the doctor put a hand on Ray's shoulder. "One of the best things you can do is stay positive about your future. If you decide to go through with chemotherapy, it helps a lot of people mentally—just knowing you're doing something to prevent the cancerous cells from spreading."

"What would you do if you were me?"

Dr. Contos scratched his jaw, conflicting emotions surfacing across his face. "I'd trust that my doctor has my best interest in mind."

"I need to talk to my kids and then I'll let you know."

"Okay." The word came out slow as if the oncologist didn't believe that was the best idea. "I hope to hear from you soon." Dr. Contos turned and left the room.

Ray nestled under the blankets and closed his eyes. That conversation had exhausted him. And he still had more hard conversations ahead. He had to talk to Amanda and Caleb again. His children were all he had left, and he wouldn't make this decision without them.

THAT NIGHT ETHAN knocked on the back door to Uncle Cameron's house. He couldn't hear any footsteps coming toward the door. Several loud, excited voices shouted at one time. Uncle Cameron had five kids, all under the age of ten. If the shouting continued, no one would hear him knocking. After talking to Ray, Ethan needed to speak with his uncle—the director of the oncology unit—to get advice.

He twisted the knob, relieved to find it open. Toy trucks and dolls were scattered across the living room floor. Cartoons played on the big screen TV at full volume. A baby swing swung back and forth, lulling his youngest cousin to sleep with classical music. No wonder Uncle Cameron enjoyed sitting alone in his office in complete silence.

The door to the bathroom swung open and his aunt stepped out, barely noticing him as she bent over and yanked a pull-up over her daughter's chunky legs. She briefly glanced at him as she shimmied sparkly pink pants over the pull-up. "*Yassoo.*"

The familiar Greek hello brought warmth to his chest. "I hope you don't mind that I came over this late. You're probably trying to get the kids ready for bed."

Standing, she waved her hand with indifference. "Elena had a dance recital tonight, so we're behind schedule. Are you hungry? We have leftover gyros in the fridge."

"That's okay. I just ate dinner at Val's Diner."

"You'll miss American food when you move back, won't you?"

He patted his stomach. "Heck yes. Valerie makes the best cheeseburgers, especially when she adds curly fries to the burger."

"Better not mention any greasy American food to your parents. They assume you're eating with us most of the time."

Ethan withheld a sigh. His parents didn't approve of most of his decisions. Growing up, he'd always been the odd one out. He was the only boy of four kids. All of his sisters loved living in a big Greek family, enjoying most of their customs. But he continued to question their traditions; the conformity often felt more like drowning.

The baby in the swing suddenly woke up, his shrill cry superseding the rest of the noise in the house.

"Is Uncle Cameron around?" Ethan asked loudly.

"He's upstairs, giving Elena a bath."

"Oh. I can come back another time."

"It's okay. Just head on up."

Ethan chuckled. To most single guys his age, the noisy chaos would be overwhelming. But when his extended relatives in Greece met for family gatherings, their boisterous conversations were no comparison to this, especially when they all talked over one another.

He stepped over a train track, a dollhouse, and a plastic drum set, and headed up the stairs to the bathroom. Uncle Cameron kneeled on a rug, pouring water over Elena's head. Shampoo washed out of her long, dark hair down into the soapy bath.

Wiping the water off her face, the four-year-old blinked and opened her eyes. "Cousin Ethan!"

Ethan smiled at her before getting down to business. "Uncle Cameron, I need to talk to you about a new patient." He leaned against the doorframe. Hopefully, his uncle would know what to do about Ray and Amanda. "The patient just had surgery today and he needs chemotherapy, but his daughter doesn't want him to do it."

"If you've already told them the facts, then all you can do is wait for your patient to make a decision." Uncle Cameron poured body soap on a small cloth and washed it over Elena's back.

"I think the patient's daughter is one of those people who only prefers natural remedies compared to medicine, but I have a feeling there's more to it than that." He'd wanted to ask Amanda yesterday, but he hadn't wanted to make her more upset.

Elena thrust her hands in front of her dad's face. "My fingers are all wrinkly. Can I get out now?"

Nodding, Uncle Cameron lifted Elena out of the tub and wrapped her in a towel. "Why don't you go to your room and pick out pajamas? I'll be there in a minute."

"Okie-dokie."

His uncle pulled the drain and stood. "It sounds like you're starting to care about these people. I wouldn't suggest befriending patients and their family members. It's not wise to get too invested in their lives."

"It's not that easy. My patient and his daughter live here."

"Oh." Uncle Cameron's voice raised an octave higher. "We don't get many oncology patients from Maple Valley, but I had a patient from here a few years ago."

"Did you know the person well?"

"Yes. Michelle Miller was a friend of mine. She was the assistant principal of the elementary school. I'd see her at every school event. Our kids were also in the same sports, so we spent a lot of time together at soccer games. When she was diagnosed with cancer, I couldn't stop being friends with her and she refused to see any other doctor."

"So you made it work."

Uncle Cameron pulled the shower curtain closed, a faraway look in his eyes. "I did everything I could to save her life. But after battling lung cancer for three years, she passed away. A patient's death has never affected me so hard. For the first time in my career, I had to take time off work."

Ethan's chest tightened. His uncle made a good point. Losing a patient was hard enough—several of his patients in Greece had passed away. He couldn't imagine losing a friend or relative that he'd treated.

His watch beeped at the turn of the hour. He glanced

down. "I should get going so you can get the kids to sleep."

"Before you go, there's something I want to tell you." Uncle Cameron picked up Elena's discarded dress from the floor. "I spoke with your mom earlier."

Dread settled in the pit of his stomach. What had Mom said this time? Had she complained that Ethan was running away from his problems?

Uncle Cameron twisted the dress in his hands. "Your dad heard rumors that Raechel's family wants to end the business merger and split Poseidonas into two separate companies again."

Ethan gritted his teeth. Fifty years ago, Pappous had started his own fishing company, dreaming of making it a family business. Many people in their family worked for the company. The fishing business was their livelihood, especially for his parents.

"Do you think Raechel has anything to do with this?" his uncle asked.

"She might. We didn't end on good terms and this could be her way of getting back at me." But he'd never imagined his ex-wife taking it this far. She needed to get her emotions under control and realize how beneficial the merger was. Since their families had gone into business together, the fishing company's sales had skyrocketed.

Uncle Cameron leaned against the bathroom vanity.

"Will you tell me what happened between you two?"

"Does it matter? We aren't together anymore, and she's getting remarried soon."

"Just because she's marrying someone else doesn't erase the unresolved issues between you." Uncle Cameron crossed his arms. "And it would help everyone understand what you're going through."

"Not everyone in our family needs to know all the details of my life." He expected his uncle to respond argumentatively, but Uncle Cameron chuckled instead. "What's so funny?"

"You're so much like me. I moved to the US because I saw a greater need for oncologists, but living far away from our family sure has its benefits."

Ethan smiled. "Yes, it does. They have no idea what my life is like here, and they can't question everything I do."

Nodding, Uncle Cameron pushed off the bathroom vanity. "I better get Elena to bed. I'll see you at work tomorrow."

"Okay." Ethan descended the stairs. Had Raechel convinced her dad to end the merger? She had a hot and cold personality, and when she wanted to be cold, she could stay cold for a long time.

She hadn't always been that way. At least, not at first. They'd been friends since they were young, so dating had been easy—no awkward or nervous moments, or fights.

But their relationship had spiraled downhill as soon as they got married. They started trying to conceive, dreaming of a big Greek family. No one else in their families had infertility issues, so they'd expected it to be easy, like everything else in their relationship.

Year after year went by with no signs of a baby. After trying fertility drugs and artificial insemination, their relationship was strained. They fought constantly with no end in sight. One argument led to another until they could barely look at each other without contempt.

All of Raechel's anger was directed at him. She wanted someone to blame.

What he hadn't realized in the beginning was how far Raechel would go to have a baby.

Chapter 6

AMANDA TRUDGED INTO the Maple Valley Community Center, carrying a banana ginger smoothie. She'd barely slept, tossing and turning until early morning sunlight poured through her window.

The house had been too quiet without Dad. No reruns of *Deadliest Catch* blaring from the TV, or loud tinkering coming from the attached garage, or their greyhound's barking as Dad played tug-of-war with Hank.

But it wasn't just the quiet house that had kept her heart racing late into the night. It was a million 'what if' questions terrorizing her every thought. How much longer did Dad have left to live? What would the next few years be like for him? Would he suffer? The unknown haunted her peaceful rest, until she'd given up on sleep altogether and called to check on him.

Hearing his voice had brought her heart rate back to a steady beat. He'd sounded good, reassuring her that he would be fine and he'd see her later, after she went to the

Maple Valley Community Committee meeting.

She walked toward the back of the building and stepped inside a large room with a long oval table. A few committee members stood near the coffee machine with Styrofoam cups, while others lingered next to a folding table filled with sweets from Candy Galore.

Several heads turned in her direction, sending sympathetic looks. It hadn't taken long for everyone in Maple Valley to hear about Dad.

Amanda tilted her head back and took a long drink of her smoothie. The pity in their eyes looked all too familiar. She didn't want people to feel sorry for her. But she did appreciate their support. People had already started bringing over meals.

Kendall tossed a sugar-covered gummy worm into her mouth and rushed across the room. She flung her arms around Amanda, her growing belly pushing into Amanda's torso. "How's Coach?"

"He's doing well. He was just moved out of the ICU." Amanda ran a hand through her loose curls, frowning. "But Ethan wants my dad to do chemo."

Kendall stroked Amanda's forearm. "Furnam Hospital is nationally ranked. Your dad is in the right place. And if anyone can beat cancer, it's Coach."

"Thanks," Amanda said quietly.

"Wait a minute." Kendall's eyes grew big. "*Ethan* is your dad's doctor? As in, the Greek god?"

"The one and only." Sarcasm saturated her tone. She would never see Ethan the same way Kendall did. Especially after he'd done exactly what she'd asked him not to do. She was so disappointed. And yet, she had to admit that he was just doing his job. What she'd asked of him *was* unfair. But Ethan hadn't seen the way Mom had suffered.

Kendall looked over Amanda's shoulder.

Turning, Amanda followed Kendall's gaze to see Tyler walking inside the room, dressed in light jeans and a navy blue sweater.

Her stomach knotted into a tight ball. He looked like an Abercrombie model. The sweater brought out the blue hues in his eyes. The jeans fit snugly against his hips. His clean-shaven face accented his hard jawline.

Kendall nudged Amanda with her elbow. "You're staring," she whispered.

Ugh. Tyler wasn't hers anymore. He didn't get ready this morning thinking about her. Not when he'd picked out a shirt, or shaved his face, or gelled his hair. But maybe he'd never considered her in the first place. She'd assumed he had because she'd always thought of him.

Disgust rose to the back of her throat. Five wasted years of putting Tyler on a pedestal. Believing he was the one. Dreaming about a future together.

She tipped the banana smoothie against her lips, taking another long drink as Tyler stopped in front of her. "I'm sorry to hear about your dad. Are you okay?"

Between Tyler and Dad, how could she possibly be okay? She bit back the retort, recognizing sadness in his eyes that mirrored her own feelings. Tyler had spent a lot of time getting to know Dad. "I'm holding up."

"Let's get started." Jason Donovon, the president of the committee, moved to the front of the room, near the whiteboard. He waited for everyone to sit before continuing. "In the next few months, we need to plan the following fall events: the pumpkin patch, haunted house, health fair, and of course, our fall festival. I need each of you to sign up for two events. I'll pass around little slips of paper. Put your name on one and list two events."

Amanda tapped her pen against the table. She'd always volunteered with Tyler, planning the haunted house and pumpkin patch. This year, she'd pick the health fair and fall festival.

Kendall leaned over, peeking at Amanda's paper and scribbling the same events.

Picking up the papers, Jason quickly wrote the names of members on the board. He wrote left-handed, blocking each list until he moved on to the next event. He moved away from the health fair and started writing the next list.

Tyler hadn't signed up for it. Her shoulders lowered with relief. Volunteering with him would be like tearing a Band-Aid off a fresh, bleeding wound.

A minute later, his name showed up under the haunted house, but not the pumpkin patch, which only left one event. Jason finished the list for the fall festival, writing *Amanda* and *Tyler* among several others.

She chewed on the tip of her smoothie straw. *Ugh.*

Jason stepped back, scanning the board. "The haunted house has the longest list and the health fair has the least. I need a few people from the haunted house to switch to the health fair."

Dill, the manager of the local grocery store, and Sandy, the owner of Candy Galore, both raised their hands.

"Thank you. I'd still like to have at least one more person." His gaze roamed over the table, falling on Tyler. "Since you're a chiropractor, would you mind switching? You'd be a great asset."

Tyler nodded slowly. "Sure …"

Using her thumb, Amanda wiped away the perspiration sliding down her smoothie bottle. His hesitancy twisted her stomach into knots like the worst labor pains she could imagine. Even though *she* didn't want to volunteer with him, her reasoning was different than his. He was the one who'd asked for a break. The one who had her second-guessing everything they'd shared.

AMANDA DROPPED HER yoga mat by the front door. The brisk morning had kept all of the birth center's patients from showing up to her yoga class in the park. She'd have to switch to afternoons when the temperature was warmest.

She pulled her hair up into a ponytail and switched into her tennis shoes. She'd go for a run instead. She needed to do something to wear off the anxious energy coursing through her body. Would Dad do chemo or not? When he'd returned home from the hospital, he still hadn't made a decision. He'd called her twin brother last night, talking to him for over an hour. Caleb thought Dad should do it.

But Caleb wouldn't be here to watch Dad's body deteriorate from poisonous toxins. Sometimes she wondered if her brother would ever come home for good. If it hadn't been for his high school sweetheart leaving him, he'd probably still live in Maple Valley. Caleb and Grace would probably be married with a growing family. But Grace had broken his heart. She'd moved away without a word, deactivated her social media accounts, changed her phone number, and never returned. Her absence still stung, for both Amanda and Caleb.

Amanda finished tying her tennis shoes and stood, noticing the silence. Their lanky greyhound slid off the couch and ambled toward her, wagging his tail. She patted the top of his gray-colored head while scanning the empty living room. "Hey, Hank. Where's Dad?"

Hank stuck his tongue out and licked his nose. Slobber dripped onto the wood floor.

"You're no help." She scratched behind his ears for a moment, the silence in the house deafening. "Dad?"

No answer.

She rushed past Hank, checking Dad's bedroom and the bathroom. Both were empty. "Dad?" Her voice shook. He'd been feeling much better after surgery, but what if he'd fallen?

She jogged into the kitchen. An almost empty plate of egg whites and fruit sat on the table. A pot of coffee had recently been brewed, the fresh scent of warm coffee grounds filling the room.

If he wasn't in the house, he must be in the garage or out on the dock. Her stomach coiled. What if he'd fainted and fell into the water? She yanked the sliding glass door open. Voices and laughter echoed across the backyard.

Weird. She walked farther into the yard and peered down the hill. Near the bank of the river, Dad and Ethan sat in Dad's fishing boat. Dad held a net in his hand as Ethan reeled in a fish.

What was Ethan doing here? Amanda stopped midstride. Tyler had gone fishing with Dad once. But he'd only come back annoyed at sitting around all day.

She hadn't encouraged him to go again. She wasn't the type of girl to hopelessly try to change a guy. Tyler didn't have a lot in common with Dad, but at least he'd made an effort.

She walked down the slope, stepping onto the dock. The wood creaked beneath her tennis shoes.

Dad looked up from the fish dangling on Ethan's hook. Meeting her gaze, he took off his fishing hat and fiddled with it. "I, uh … I thought you taught yoga this morning."

"No one showed up." She walked to the end of the dock, staring at Ethan. He wore tattered blue jeans and a red and black plaid shirt with the sleeves rolled up to his elbows. His thick hair was slightly disheveled from the wind, blown back away from his forehead. Her stomach did an unexpected, airy summersault. "What are you doing here?"

He shrugged. "Your dad invited me." With his attention on her, the fish flapped wildly in the air before detaching from the hook. It dropped back into the murky river with a flop.

Dad slapped his leg with fervor. "Ah, come on! That was Ethan's first catch in the Mississippi."

She frowned. "Should you be fishing on your boat right now? You could tear your incision."

Ethan reeled in the empty line. "I checked the incision before we got in the boat. As long as he doesn't make any jerky movements, he'll be fine."

Her attraction fizzled as she realized what Ethan's motives had to be. "Are you fishing with my dad just so you can convince him to do treatment?"

Dad gripped the handle of the net tightly. "Young lady, that's no way to treat a guest."

Heat traveled up her ears. How embarrassing, being treated like a child in front of Ethan.

"It's okay, Ray." Ethan looked up at her, his expression serious. "I like to fish. Your dad likes to fish. End of story."

"So you haven't talked about treatment?" she asked quietly.

"No."

She took a step back, assessing his response. It seemed like he was telling the truth. "I'm going for a run."

"You could join us if you want."

All she'd done was accuse him, and he wanted to spend time with her? If only Tyler felt the same way. Then again, maybe Ethan was just trying to be nice in an awkward situation.

Standing, Ethan held out his hand, palm up. His creamy chocolate eyes lit with the hint of a dare. "I promise not to dunk you in the river, but only if you promise the same. What do you say?"

Amanda took another step back. Ethan was quite the

charmer. No wonder he had so many women wrapped around his finger. But no way would that ever be her. "Some other time. Have fun."

SITTING DOWN, ETHAN baited his hook with a live worm and cast the line into the river. The hook disappeared below the surface and slow, circular ripples glided across the dark water. He glanced up at the log cabin. A few minutes ago, he'd seen Amanda run off on a trail along the river.

He'd tried not to stare, but Ray had caught him looking and Ethan had forced his gaze to return to the river. At least her dad couldn't hear his thoughts. Amanda had a great body—athletic, yet curvy in all the rights spots. Every step showcased her trim, lean legs.

His line tugged beneath the water. He reeled it in a little, seeing if the fish would follow. The tugging continued. He reeled in the line a little more.

Ray pulled a tackle box onto his lap, noticeably wincing.

"Are you okay?"

"Yeah, it hurts when I bend over sometimes."

"Let me help you next time. I don't want you to overdo it. If you get tired of being out here, we can stop."

"Are you kidding? This is the best I've felt since my surgery. Nothing is stopping me today."

Ethan nodded. As a doctor, he wanted to tell Ray that fishing wasn't worth tearing an incision, but the fisherman in him decided to stay quiet. Pappous always said that fishing was good for the soul, and right now, it seemed to be just what Ray needed. If the old man showed any signs of serious pain, Ethan would draw the line then.

Ray lifted a plastic worm out of the box and baited his line. "You got a girlfriend?"

Ethan chuckled at the sudden change of conversation. "No, sir."

"Just so you know, Amanda's single."

"Oh." He wanted to add: I'm aware of that because *she hit me with her car after the breakup*, but judging from the look of panic on Amanda's face when Ray had questioned them, he surmised she hadn't told her dad.

"Amanda and Tyler are over. She's waiting for him to change his mind, but I don't want her to date him again."

Ethan held back a smile. So Ray was playing matchmaker now.

"I just thought you should know." Turning toward the river, Ray cast his line into the water. "So, what made you want to become an oncologist?"

The tugging grew harder. Ethan stood, slowly reeling. "My sister was diagnosed with leukemia when she was ten."

Ray's fishing pole drooped slightly. "Is she okay now?"

"Yeah. Sophia's been in remission for fifteen years."

"Did she do chemotherapy?"

Ethan nodded. "Sophia lost her hair, threw up all the time, and missed a lot of school. But it saved her life."

"If I do it, will you be the one overseeing my treatment?"

Ethan stopped reeling. He'd told Amanda today was only about fishing and he'd intended to keep his word. And yet, if Ray wanted to talk about treatment, Ethan wouldn't stop him. "Yes."

"My business partner's newborn just got home from the hospital a few days ago. She had part of her lung removed."

Ethan tilted his head slightly, trying to figure out where this conversation was going. "Is the baby okay now?"

"She's perfectly fine." Ray looked down at the river and ran a hand over his beard. "It's amazing to think how skilled the surgeon and anesthesiologist must've been to operate on a newborn."

"I'm very impressed with the staff at Furnam. I've learned a lot while I've worked there."

Ray glanced in Ethan's direction, studying him behind his Coke-bottle glasses. "I've made my decision."

Ethan gripped his fishing pole. *Come to your senses, Ray. It could save your life.*

"I'd like to give chemo a go."

"I'm happy to hear that." Ethan bit back a smile. Ray might have a chance, and Ethan had the opportunity to save him. He started reeling again, bringing the fish so close to the water's surface he could see the fins.

"I saw how you and Amanda were looking at each other. I'm sure she'll visit me when I go in for treatment. It would be good for her to spend time with you."

Huh? Ethan almost dropped his fishing pole. "Please tell me that's not why you're doing chemo."

"No, it's not, but it's an added benefit. Amanda's ex-boyfriend broke things off and then I got diagnosed with cancer. She's going through a lot right now, and you are the perfect distraction." Ray lifted his chin and smiled. "In fact, I think it'd be nice if you hung out together outside of the hospital."

Ethan scratched the back of his head, Uncle Cameron's warning returning all too quickly. *Don't befriend patients and their family members. Don't get too invested in their lives.* Ethan had already gone fishing with Ray, and now the old man wanted him to date Amanda?

He couldn't, not only because he was Ray's doctor, but also because he had three more months in the US. He hadn't dated anyone seriously over the last few years, and he sure wasn't about to start now—maybe never.

And after he moved back to Greece, he'd hopefully make amends with his parents. He couldn't fix their relationship if he dated a non-Greek woman. His traditional parents would disown him. "Ray … I can't date your daughter. I'm moving home soon and that wouldn't be fair to her."

Ray chuckled. "Look, you seem like a good guy, but that's not what I was asking. Just hang out. Have fun together."

"I'm not so sure that's a good idea."

"Trust me, it is." Winking, Ray reeled in his line, acting as if the conversation was over.

Ethan opened his mouth to tell Ray "no," then decided against it. Ray had just decided to do chemo. Ethan couldn't make his new patient angry, in case it would change Ray's mind. And now that Ray wanted to do chemo, Amanda would probably blame Ethan. She wouldn't want to hang out with him anyway. Better to wait and let it all play out.

Chapter 7

AMANDA DRUMMED HER fingers along the armrest of her chair. She crossed her legs, then uncrossed them. Still restless, she rummaged through the contents of her cluttered purse. Now would be a good time to clean it out—anything to distract her from looking at the room full of patients undergoing chemotherapy.

She pulled out a receipt for Val's Diner, protein bar wrappers, and a movie ticket for *Fall in Love*. She glanced up to look for a garbage can.

Big mistake. Her gaze locked on a middle-aged woman sitting across the room. The woman leaned back in a reclining chair. Her cheekbones protruded above sunken skin and dark bags hung beneath her eyes as she stared blankly at one of the big screen TVs hanging from the ceiling.

Waves of nausea rolled through Amanda's stomach. That could be Dad soon. She tossed the wrappers, ticket, and receipt back into her purse and grabbed her flowery billfold. She had to get out of here before she had another panic attack.

She rose from her chair. "Do you need anything? I'm going to the cafeteria."

Dad lowered the *Maple Valley Tribune* to his lap. "How about a juicy steak? Medium rare."

She put her hands on her hips. How could he joke at a time like this? "I'm serious."

"A coffee sounds good, Minnow."

"Okay." Caffeine wasn't the healthiest option for him, but she would do anything to make him comfortable right now. Heck, maybe she'd get a cup too. She'd woken up several times last night, wondering how his first round of treatment would go. "I'll be right back."

"No rush. I'm reading about the new football coach at Stetson Academy. They've won three games in a row."

"Sounds like they might be the team to beat this year."

"Yuppers." He lifted the paper until she could no longer see his face. Her gaze drifted to the IV sticking out of his forearm. Fluid dripped through the tube, administering chemo into his body.

She shuddered. All those toxins were killing off his healthy cells. Part of her wanted to rip out the IV, but she wouldn't. She had to support Dad's decision. Keeping up his morale would be important too.

But now that he'd made a choice, she had new concerns. Like how they'd pay for treatment. Before Mom's death, her parents hadn't bought life insurance, so Dad had spent most of their savings on Mom's funeral. Thankfully, he had bought life insurance since then. But any treatment he needed now would be expensive.

Leaving the oncology unit, she took the stairs two at a time, eager for new scenery. She walked past a gift shop and a library before entering the cafeteria. Several people stood in line carrying trays filled with pancakes, waffles, omelets, and sausages.

She poured two black coffees, paid, and turned around to go back upstairs. "Oomph!" One of the coffees dropped out of her hand, splashing against the person she'd smashed into, then spilled onto the floor.

She took a step back, watching Ethan yank the fabric away from his chest as a dark stain seeped into his green scrubs.

She cupped a hand over her mouth, mumbling an apology as he continued to tug at his shirt, lifting the V-neck away from his chest and revealing light brown hairs.

Her lips parted. Ethan was much different from Tyler, who shaved his face and chest the second he saw any hair. She'd always liked the clean-cut look, but catching sight of Ethan's chest caused heat to flame beneath her cheeks. A little chest hair was surprisingly sexy.

Ethan gave her a sideways grin. "I'm starting to wonder if you're purposely trying to hurt me."

Amanda made a *hmpf* noise. She grabbed a napkin and dabbed it on his shirt. "Maybe you have a habit of getting in my way." They exchanged a long look, her words carrying a heavier meaning.

"Just so you know, your dad made the decision without me."

She dabbed harder at the spot.

Ethan sighed. He covered her hand with his, holding it still. "Why are you against chemo? Besides the side effects, I mean."

Her chest rose and fell at his touch and sent little electric jolts down her spine. "I think the long list of side effects are enough of a reason."

"But they aren't the only reason, are they?"

Amanda moved her hand out of his grasp and fiddled with the locket on her necklace. Unwilling to meet his steady gaze, she kneeled down to wipe the coffee off the floor.

Ethan grabbed a stack of napkins and kneeled next to her, helping. "Why do you reach for that locket every time I bring up a hard topic?"

She stiffened. "I do?"

Ethan nodded.

She cleaned the last of the coffee from the floor, then picked up the empty cup and stood to throw it away. When Ethan moved to a standing position, she finally met his gaze. "It was my mom's necklace."

"Was?" he asked in a quiet tone.

"She died when I was a senior in high school." A lump formed in her throat. "I suppose the necklace makes me feel closer to her. Stupid, I know."

"No, it's not." Ethan shook his head, his dark eyes full of compassion.

Amanda held her breath, waiting for him to press further, but he didn't. "I need to ask you something too."

"What is it?"

"Who should I talk to about financial aid?"

Ethan ran a hand over the stubble on his jaw, a flash of disappointment surfacing across his face.

Had he wanted her to open up more about her mom?

"You could meet with one of our social workers. We have several payment plans and financial aid options. I can give you more information later when I check on your dad."

"Thank you."

"You could also talk to the social worker about how you're coping with your dad's diagnosis." He opened his mouth, then closed it as if he was afraid to say what was on his mind. "And you could talk about your mom."

Amanda nodded and held up the other coffee in her hand. "I should get back upstairs before this gets cold."

"Did you go to a counselor after your mom passed away?"

"No."

"Don't tell me you're against therapists, too."

She slid her tongue across her teeth, making a clicking noise. "Not exactly." She hadn't felt the need to go to a counselor. After Mom died, Amanda's best friend, Grace, had literally been her saving grace. They'd spent hours on the phone or at each other's houses. Grace had known when to listen and when to comfort her with words. Grace had even encouraged her to pursue meditation, a practice that had saved her sanity. Without Grace's support, Amanda would've crumbled.

Ethan gently touched her elbow. "Just so you know, in addition to medical treatment, I believe that patients should eat healthier, get massages, do acupuncture, etc. All of those can relieve symptoms. It doesn't have to be one way or the other. We can find a good combination. With both of us helping him, your dad will have the best care possible."

She bit the side of her bottom lip. Ethan made it sound like they were a team. As if that was possible. Her career was based on encouraging patients to trust their natural instincts and believe in the strength of the human body. She'd never imagined teaming up with an oncologist, who frequently encouraged patients to use invasive medicine. And she'd never pictured herself siding with a man like Ethan—someone she found equally attractive and frustrating at the exact same time.

He let go of her elbow, never taking his eyes off of her. "I have your dad's best interest at heart. I promise."

He seemed so confident that part of her wanted to lean into his arms and let him hold her. Let him tell her that everything would be okay. But the reality of the situation wasn't that simple.

Instead, she forced her feet to move out of the cafeteria, away from Ethan and his promises.

NEARING THE SOCIAL worker's room, Amanda tucked a folded piece of paper inside her purse. She'd prepared a list of questions to ask. Some of her questions were about Dad's finances and how they could pay for treatment. She'd also added a few questions about how she could help him cope. Above all else, that was most important.

She stopped outside of the social worker's door and knocked. No one answered. She knocked again. "Marissa Peyton?"

Behind her, another door opened. "Marissa had a family emergency. She just left. But I'm free if you want to meet with me instead."

Amanda's pulse pounded in her ears. She would know that voice anywhere. She slowly turned around, coming face-to-face with the woman she thought she'd never see again.

Grace took a step back, her childhood friend's eyes widening. All the color drained from her face. "Oh my God."

Amanda tried to respond, but her mouth was suddenly dry, making it hard to speak. She blinked, just to make sure her eyes weren't playing tricks on her.

After ten years apart, the girlish face she had once known was gone, replaced by the slim contours of a woman. Grace's dark brown hair was pulled back into a tight braid, exposing her high cheekbones and slender nose. She'd rarely worn makeup in high school, but today she wore a rose-colored lipstick and a pale pink eye color to match.

Grace noticeably swallowed. "What are you doing here?"

"I, uh ... My dad has cancer. Ethan ... I mean, Dr. Contos suggested I see a social worker."

"Oh no." Grace put a hand over her chest. "How are you doing?"

Amanda shifted her weight from one foot to the other. It felt oddly familiar to hear the concern in Grace's tone, as if all those years apart hadn't happened at all. "I'm still in shock, I guess."

"That's understandable."

Amanda doubted that most people felt as shocked as she did right now. In this moment, it had nothing to do with Dad and everything to do with seeing Grace.

She adjusted the purse strap on her shoulder. "Do you want to grab a snack from the cafeteria? I'd love to catch up."

"I'm not so sure that's a good idea."

Amanda crossed her arms, stung by the rejection. Grace was the one who had run off. What could Amanda have done to make her so guarded?

Grace started to close the door to her office. "I'm sure you'll get a call from Marissa to reschedule your appointment."

Amanda pursed her lips. So this was how Grace wanted to act. To pretend they didn't have a past. "Caleb's in the air force now. He loves it."

Grace set her long braid in front of her shoulder, running her fingers along the end. "That's great."

"He's deployed to Iraq right now."

Grace's eyebrows pinched together. "Oh."

"He misses you. We both do. We didn't know what happened to you. Did you ever think about that?" Amanda's voice shook as she searched Grace's expression. "Do you even care?"

"Of course … I still care about Caleb and you."

"Why didn't you call us after you moved, then?"

"I wanted to. You have no idea how many times I picked up the phone, but I could never bring myself to call."

Amanda bit back an angry reply. Grace had been her

best friend since kindergarten. They'd played the same games at recess in elementary school; in junior high, they'd been locker buddies; as teenagers, they'd spent most weekends shopping at the mall or watching romantic comedies at the theater. Until Grace moved away, they'd shared every secret, doubt, and dream. "No matter what happened, I would've been there for you. I thought our friendship meant something to you."

"It did." Grace looked away as if shutting out her thoughts. As if shutting out Amanda. Again.

"Oh right. That's what friends do—leave without a word." Anxiety about Dad mixed with the pain and confusion of suddenly confronting Grace caused a tangle of emotions to twist inside Amanda's chest.

Grace's cheeks now matched the color of her rose-colored lipstick. "I don't want to talk about it right now."

The simple refusal stopped Amanda and took the fight right out of her. Despite their childhood connection, Grace was a grown adult who didn't owe Amanda an explanation. And she couldn't judge Grace's actions when she didn't even know the circumstances. "Fine," Amanda said quietly. "If you ever want to tell me, I would still be here for you."

Grace sent her a weak smile. "Thanks."

Amanda turned and strode down the hallway, almost shaking. She'd imagined this moment so many times, but she'd hoped it would be Grace reaching out to her. Grace finally explaining why she'd left.

"HOW DID THE appointment with Amanda go yesterday?" Ethan leaned against the doorframe of Marissa's office. He shouldn't ask, due to HIPPA laws, but Marissa would only give him a vague answer anyway. And he'd been wondering all day.

"I haven't met with her yet. My brother's appendix almost burst and I had to leave early."

"Oh."

Grace opened her door and stepped out into the hallway. "I spoke with Amanda. I told her you'd reschedule."

"Thanks." Marissa smiled. "Well, I need to get some work done. I have a lot of catching up to do." She turned back into her office and shut the door.

Ethan walked closer to Grace's office, keeping his voice quiet. "I wanted to put Amanda on your schedule; I think you would work well with her, but you've taken a lot of time off lately. I didn't want to overwhelm you."

Grace looked down at her hand, flicking coral nail polish off her fingernails. "She can't be my client anyway."

"Why not?"

"We grew up together."

"Were you friends?"

"Yes." Grace turned back into her office.

He followed her inside, watching as she put a stack of papers into a desk drawer, then locked it. He normally didn't pry, but knowing they had grown up together fueled the spark of his curiosity. Maybe he wasn't so different from his nosy family after all. "I take it you're not friends anymore."

Grace glanced down at a picture frame on her desk and shook her head.

Ethan waited for her to respond, but she remained quiet. Grace was a hard person to read. She'd started working at Furnam Hospital a few months ago, and he knew very little about her, except that she'd moved from Missouri to help her mom open a bed-and-breakfast.

He sat on the edge of her desk, fiddling with a pen. "Amanda is having a hard time with her dad's decision to do chemo. I think it's bringing back a lot of painful memories of her mom."

Grace's head jerked up. "I can only imagine. I don't know how Amanda feels now, but in high school, she blamed herself for Barbara's death."

"Why?"

"She was supposed to come home right after school that afternoon, but she stayed to play volleyball with some other girls." Grace twisted her hands together and tucked her chin close to her chest. "When she got home, she found Barbara on the bathroom floor, barely breathing."

He dropped the pen, letting it land on Grace's desk with a light thud. "That must've been terrifying."

She nodded.

"What happened to her mom? Was she sick?" Ethan tugged at his earlobe. The decent thing to do would've been to wait and ask Amanda, but the question had been on the tip of his tongue since he'd last spoken to Amanda.

Grace licked her lips. "You don't know?"

He shook his head.

She stared at the wall behind him, a distant, empty look clouding her eyes. "Barbara swallowed a handful of her antidepressant pills."

His eyebrows rose. He couldn't begin to process how hard that must've been for Amanda, especially as a teenager. No wonder she didn't like traditional medicine. Her mom had used it to take her own life.

AMANDA SNAPPED A blank paper onto a clipboard and drew an outline of Bishop's Farm as she admired the beautiful landscape. Tall oak trees with orange and red leaves were scattered across the expanse of land, covering some of the barn, farmhouse, and silo in shade. Just beyond the barn, a corn maze weaved through a yellowed cornfield.

At the last fall festival meeting, she'd suggested they try a new location, like Bishop's Farm. People around here liked to keep things the same. She was usually one of them, but after her breakup, she was in the mood for a change. She hadn't thought anyone would agree to a new location for the festival, and at first, many people had been hesitant, but they'd finally relented.

She tapped the pencil against her lips as she pictured where each station would go.

Tyler's Mercedes rumbled along the gravel driveway, kicking up dust.

Dread settled in the pit of her stomach. She hadn't seen him since their fall festival meeting a week ago. He'd been very aloof and quiet, making it clear that he didn't want to volunteer with her.

He stepped out of his car, wearing dress pants, a cashmere sweater, and aviators. She glanced down at her clipboard, pretending to be preoccupied. His sense of style never ceased to impress her.

As he drew near, his dress shoes crunched along the gravel. "Hi."

She looked up. "Hey."

Several snorts and squeaks filled the silence before a dozen pigs sauntered out of the barn toward their breakfast. If she had been standing with anyone else, she would've laughed. But she couldn't. It wasn't supposed to be this awkward between them.

Kendall's Jeep sped down the driveway and parked beside Amanda's car. Relief spread through Amanda. She didn't have to be alone with Tyler any longer.

Getting out of her Jeep, Kendall walked forward with Sandy and Mark beside her. A striped maternity top accented her belly, which suddenly looked more like a ball than a bump. "My alarm didn't go off this morning. Did we miss anything? What do we need to do?"

Amanda put her arm around Kendall's shoulders. "For someone just entering your third trimester, you have so much energy."

Sandy shook her head, sending white bangs across her forehead. "You're tellin' me. Mark and I couldn't get a word in."

Mark grunted. "If you ask me, she must've put a few energy shots in that tea of hers."

Kendall put a hand on her ample chest, acting offended. "Who picked you up? Oh, that's right. I did. You're welcome." Winking, she turned back to Amanda. "And my energy level won't be like this all day, so let's get to work. What's first on the agenda?"

"We need to decide where to put each station. Last year they had face painting, bobbing for apples, pumpkin carving, a food vendor, and a corn maze. We also need to look at the barn and decide where to put the dance floor, beer tent, and food tables."

"I can help you with the outside stations," Kendall said.

"Great." Now Amanda could tell her about running into Grace. The three of them had spent a lot of time together in high school. Kendall would be shocked.

Tyler widened his stance and squared his shoulders. "Kendall, would you mind looking at the barn? I can help Amanda with the stations."

What? Amanda exchanged a panicked look with Kendall, but her friend shrugged.

Sandy looked from Tyler to Amanda. "Mark and I can help Kendall. Right, old man?"

Mark shook his head and turned toward the barn with Sandy and Kendall following at his heels. As soon as they were out of earshot, Tyler peered over his sunglass-es, surveying the farm. "This place is perfect."

"Before my parents built their riverfront home, my dad used to take Caleb and me fishing here. George Bishop has a pond behind the barn." Amanda peered up at him, squinting in the sunlight. "Is there a reason you wanted to help me? At our last meeting, it seemed like you didn't want to work together at all."

"Don't be offended, but over the weekend, I over-heard your dad talking to his friends at Val's Diner. It sounds like he's worried about paying for treatment."

Amanda pursed her lips. She'd met with Marissa Peyton yesterday. Dad made too much money to receive financial aid. And even with a monthly payment plan, the bills would significantly cut into his savings.

She dug her shoe into the gravel. "I don't see why this concerns you. We aren't dating anymore." Even though she'd kept her tone even, she noticed Tyler bristle.

"I have a solution," he said.

Her eyes widened. "What is it?"

"We could have a fundraiser."

"We?"

"The committee. We could host an event to raise money." He gave her a satisfied smile. "I know you're busy, so I'd be happy to be the one to organize it."

She shook her head in shock. Moisture built in her eyes. Her chest rose and fell, swelling with gratitude. "I don't understand. Why do you want to do this?"

Tyler took off his sunglasses, showcasing the intensity in his dark blue eyes. "I still care about you."

Her heart leapt a little, but as his words sunk in, she let her guarded walls rise. "First, you ask for a break, then you tell me you care about me. Which is it?" she asked quietly.

"Just because I asked for a break doesn't mean I stopped caring about you."

Amanda gripped the edges of the clipboard. She

didn't want to offend him after the kind offer he'd just made, but she needed to know for her own sanity. "Are you seeing other women? Is that why you wanted a break?"

"No." His answer came out rushed and sharp as if he couldn't believe she'd asked.

"Is there any chance we'll get back together?"

He drew closer and ran his fingers through her hair, playing with the loose curls. "I have some things I need to figure out, but yes."

She closed her eyes for a brief moment. His familiar touch was comforting, like lounging in front of a cozy fire. He still cared for her. There was a chance they could be together. But how long was she willing to wait for him to figure things out?

Chapter 8

ETHAN STRODE DOWN the hallway of the oncology unit, glancing at his smart watch. No matter how early he arrived at work, he always ran behind schedule by the end of the day. Usually, it didn't bother him. His uncle encouraged the staff to give every patient undivided attention. *Treat each patient like he or she is your only patient,* his uncle often said.

But this afternoon Ethan couldn't focus on his patients like he wanted to. He was running out of time to find an excuse. A week ago, during Ray's second round of chemo, he'd invited Ethan to come over for dinner tonight. Of course, Ray hadn't asked; he'd just told Ethan to come over. Ethan was supposed to arrive in two hours and he still needed to tell Ray that he wouldn't be there.

Ethan should've declined Ray's offer right away, but he wanted to see Amanda. He hadn't talked to her since she'd bumped into him in the hospital cafeteria, and for some inexplicable reason, he missed seeing her. But hanging out with a woman as intriguing as Amanda would only complicate the short time he had left in the US.

And yet, talking to her was much better than going on a date and having a surface level conversation. Before meeting Amanda, surface level conversations with women hadn't bothered him. Keeping things light and causal, and of course, never having too many dates with the same woman, ensured he'd never get to the stage of constant bickering as he had with Raechel.

And the more he learned about Ray and Amanda, the more he enjoyed getting to know them. But that was the problem. What if Ray didn't make it?

Ethan walked inside a large, open room, where several of his chemo patients rested in comfortable chairs. He stopped next to Lydia Evans, trying to clear his mind. "How are you feeling, Lydia?"

She glanced up from a spiral notebook and gave him a stern look. "Don't you have anything else better to do than bother me? I'm busy." She held the look a moment longer before a smile spread across her ashen face.

Ethan pressed the stethoscope against her heart, hearing a steady beat. "What are you writing?"

"It's a letter to my husband. Every year for our anniversary, we write each other love letters. He'll be here soon and I'm not done with mine yet."

"Happy anniversary."

"Thank you. We've been married for twenty-one years."

"Wow." Twenty-one years of marriage was impressive but seemingly daunting too. His own three years of marriage had felt like a lifetime. Looking back, he realized he'd married Raechel more because his family had wanted him to, rather than believing they were right for one another. "That's a lot of letters. How do you find something new to write about every year?"

Lydia clipped the cap of her pen onto the spiral of her notebook. "Some years I've described my favorite moments together; other years I've listed all the reasons I appreciate him." Her face grew somber and the frown lines around her mouth deepened. "This year I'm telling him what I regret the most."

"Oh." He removed the stethoscope from his ears and positioned it around his neck.

Lydia leaned her head back against the recliner. Thin strands of hair fell around her sallow cheeks. "We didn't spend enough quality time together. We were always so busy with our kids and our careers. But being diagnosed with cancer a second time …" She drew in a rapid breath and let it out slowly. "It's changed me. Each moment I spend with him is precious because I know our time may be limited."

He put two fingers on her wrist to check her pulse, wishing he could reassure Lydia that her time wasn't limited, but there was a very good chance that she was right.

Ethan glanced down at his watch. He was running out of time too. He needed to call and cancel dinner plans with the Meyers. Lydia's checkup had taken longer than he'd anticipated.

"Got a hot date later?"

He chuckled. "No, well … I haven't decided if I'm going or not."

She gave him a sidelong glance. "Is it with Ray's daughter?"

Heat rose up the back of his neck as he met Lydia's gaze. "Why would you ask that?"

"I've done outpatient chemo with Ray twice now and both times his daughter has been here with him." Lydia sent him a weak smile. "I've seen the way you look at her. What's there to think about?"

Ethan ran a hand through his hair. "It's complicated. I'm only in the US for a few more months."

"So what?" Lydia pulled the pen off of her spiral notebook and tapped it against her letter. "The things I regret most are not the things I've done. They're the things I *didn't* do. Stop living like your hourglass is running out of sand."

His lips parted. Was Lydia right? Would he regret not getting to know Amanda like he wanted to?

At the very least he could go to dinner. Surely, he'd

have more clarity after tonight.

ETHAN STOOD UNCERTAINLY on the front porch of the Meyers' cabin. Light beamed through several first-story windows, highlighting the dark wood exterior.

He held up his free hand and knocked before he could continue second-guessing his decision to bring Amanda flowers. He hoped she wouldn't read into the gesture. He'd brought her the bouquet of lilacs as a peace offering, as a way to apologize for being late.

The porch light turned on and footsteps padded toward the entrance. Amanda opened the door, looking exactly like the definition of light and casual in tight pants that accented her lean legs and a long, pink sweater. Her curly hair was tied in a messy bun with loose strands framing her face. She looked different, her expression softer than the last time they'd spoken. A hint of nervousness crossed her faced as she offered a faint smile.

Ethan swallowed, his heart thudding in response.

She stepped aside to let him in and glanced down at the flowers in his hand.

"These are for you," he said, giving them to her.

She brought the bouquet to her nose, closing her eyes for a moment. "Lilacs are my favorite. Thank you."

"Lucky guess. I've noticed you wear lilac perfume."

She lowered the bouquet, a smile spreading across her face. "No one has ever given me flowers before."

"How is that possible?" The question was out before he could think about it. What he'd meant was: how could a pretty girl like her have never received flowers?

"My dad didn't let me date in high school. He was really strict. I didn't date until college, and flowers aren't really the norm for college guys."

If *he'd* dated a woman like Amanda in college, he would've given her flowers. Not that he would tell her that.

He glanced around the large living room, searching for a new topic of conversation. Rafters decorated the high-vaulted ceilings; a bear-fur rug lay on the floor in front of a long leather couch; on the far wall, a fire flickered in a brick fireplace; dozens of photos hung above the mantel. "This place is amazing. I didn't see the inside when I came over to go fishing."

"My mom and dad had it built when my brother and I were younger."

"It reminds me of a ski lodge resort."

"They were going for the lodge look. My mom was originally from Colorado, so this was her little piece of home in Iowa."

Ethan walked over to the fireplace and looked up at the photos. Most of them included her family over the years, but one caught his attention—Amanda and a girl who looked like a younger version of Grace. The girls had their arms wrapped tightly around one another at a football game. "Is that Grace Cunningham?"

Nodding, Amanda twisted the flowers in her hands.

"Grace told me that you grew up together."

Amanda's eyes filled with a mixture of hope and pain. "What else did she tell you?"

Ethan slipped his hands inside his pockets. Amanda might be upset that Grace had told him about her mom's depression, but he had to be honest. "Well, uh …"

"What is it?"

"She told me how your mom died," he said quietly.

"Oh." Amanda noticeably swallowed.

"I'm sorry you had to lose her that way."

Amanda fiddled with the bouquet of flowers, absentmindedly plucking lilacs off the stem. "The truth is, my mom was gone long before she died. The depression medications prevented her from feeling anything."

Light from the fire flickered across Amanda's downturned her face as she continued. "The last several years of her life, my mom was alive, but she wasn't living. When my uncle died, she didn't even cry."

Amanda looked up and met his gaze. "All those pills, all those years of being numb—it was all for nothing. She took her own life before any of us could stop her."

As she continued to look at him, her expression was

serious, but not sad, her eyes filled with strength and understanding—the kind of understanding that only someone who had gone through a traumatic experience would have.

He stood still for a moment, contemplating how to respond. Amanda didn't seem like she blamed herself any longer. Instead, she seemed like a strong, independent woman, a woman who probably didn't ask for help often. Her strength drew him to her even more. He reached for her hand. His thumb caressed her palm in a slow, rhythmic motion.

She licked her lips. "Thanks for not trying to make it better, like most people do. Don't get me wrong: people mean well, but no matter what anyone says, it won't bring my mom back."

"I get it. Did your dad tell you that my sister had leukemia?"

"Yeah, he did."

"When Sophia was sick, it was obvious that our relatives felt sorry for us by what they said, and that's the last thing I wanted. More than anything, I appreciated what people did—coming to visit her at the hospital, helping her find an attractive wig, and bringing over meals for our family."

Amanda sent him a small smile. "You really do get it."

"I'm not completely hopeless." Smirking, Ethan

cupped his other hand over hers. "I'm glad you told me."

Ray strolled down the hallway, wearing sweatpants and a sweatshirt. His gray hair stuck up at odd angles and sleep lines ran across his red cheeks. He looked at Ethan. "You're late. It's about time you showed up."

Amanda gave her dad a teasing grin. "You could be a little nicer to our guest, Dad."

Ray pointed a finger at his daughter. "You of all people have no room to talk. You hit Dr. Contos with your car."

"Who told you?"

"Fern. She has a camera outside of her flower shop and caught the accident."

Amanda's cheeks turned crimson. "Who's hungry?"

Smiling, Ethan followed the pair into a long kitchen, which resembled the lodge décor of the living room with a few modern touches. It had pale blue cabinets and stainless steel appliances, but it also had the same wooden rafters on the ceiling. A chandelier resembling deer antlers hung above an ornate wooden table, which was already set.

His mouth watered as familiar Mediterranean herbs and spices intoxicated his senses, including basil, fennel, and rosemary. "Dinner smells delicious. What is it?"

"Greek chicken kabobs. I thought I'd give you a little taste of home."

His smile widened. "That was thoughtful of you."

Ray opened the fridge. "Want a beer?"

"Sure."

"I'd have one with you, but Amanda says I need to watch what I eat and drink." Ray reached for two Bud Lights, handing one to his daughter and one to Ethan as they sat down at the table.

Steam rose from their plates filled with rice and a handful of kabobs with marinated chicken, green peppers, caramelized onions, and black olives. "This looks authentic."

"Do you miss Greek food?" she asked.

"I did, at first. Now, I'm used to American food and I like it."

"Is it a lot different?"

"Yeah, there are much healthier options at the marketplaces. But the biggest difference is mealtimes." Ethan pulled an olive off of his kabob and popped one in his mouth. "In Greece, sitting down to eat a meal is a big part of our day. Here, everyone eats and moves on as if eating is a part of their to-do list."

Amanda glanced down at her plate. "I never thought about meals that way, but it's true. Sometimes, I don't eat breakfast; I make a smoothie and drink it on the go."

"When my sisters and I lived at home, my family always ate lunch together. And every Sunday, we ate lunch with my extended relatives, too."

Ray cut into his chicken. "It must be hard being

away from your family."

"It is, but sometimes I enjoy having more distance between us. My family is very nosy." Ethan took a drink of his beer. Nostalgia trickled in like an unforeseen rain. As much as he liked being so far away, he missed their boisterous conversations, contagious laughter, and constant bantering. Leaving them was the hardest decision he'd ever made. But his parents preferred his absence.

"How many sisters do you have?" Amanda asked.

"Three sisters, all married with four or five children."

"Wow, that's a lot of kids. Family get-togethers must be fun."

His stomach coiled at the wistful tone in Amanda's voice. Years ago, he'd wanted a big family too. He'd never imagined how frustrating it would be trying to conceive. "In my family, having kids is a big deal. As Americans say, the more the merrier." He took a drink of his beer. "How many siblings do you have?"

"Just my twin brother, Caleb. He's in the air force, so we only see him every three to four months between deployments."

"My son loves being in the air force. I was a soldier in Vietnam. When Caleb was little, he would look at me like I was some kind of superhero." Ray squirted soy sauce over his rice. "Of course, it doesn't feel heroic to fight in a war. Half the time, you wonder why you're there. But that sense of duty sticks with you, and when you're called out to battle, you don't bat an eyelash."

"You must be proud," Ethan said.

Amanda nodded. "We are, but selfishly, I wish he'd come home. I miss him."

"My sisters tell me that every time I talk to them."

Ray pulled the rest of the chicken and peppers off of his kabob. His tone remained nonchalant, but his eyes lit up with mischief. "Do you have anything left you'd still like to do while you're in Iowa?"

"I've heard a lot about the River Boat Cruise. I'd like to go on it before it gets too cold."

Amanda scooped rice onto her fork. "I've never done it either. I know friends who've gone and had a good time. They have a band on the boat and a dance floor." She waved her fork as she spoke, dropping some of the rice back onto her plate.

"Since Ethan is moving soon, you should show him some of our favorite spots."

Ethan almost choked on his food and he had to work to swallow it.

Amanda glared at her dad. The grandfather clock in the hallway chimed and the greyhound beside the table let out a howl. Finally, she composed herself and shrugged. "Sure, if Ethan wants to."

He tried to remember all the reasons he shouldn't hang out with Amanda, but her big, beautiful eyes waited for an answer, and all he could think about was Lydia's advice to stop living like he was in an hourglass. He wanted to have fun the next few months and Amanda would make the rest of his time in the US more enjoyable. "I'd love that."

"Great." Ray grinned and pushed his glasses higher up on his nose. "The cruise runs tomorrow night at six."

ETHAN RESTED HIS forearms above the railing of the steamboat, overlooking the Mississippi River. Down below, a large, red paddle wheel spun in circles, its rhythmic pattern in sync with the slow motion of the boat.

Waning sunlight reflected off the water, causing a shimmering glow on Amanda's face as she leaned back against the railing. A soft breeze rustled across the open deck and fluttered the bottom of her red, knee-length dress. For the first time since he'd met her, Amanda seemed completely at ease. They'd laughed and joked all throughout dinner. Her smile was contagious. Addictive. He wondered if he'd miss it when he moved.

She crossed her ankles and the heels of her boots dug into the wooden deck. "What do you think of the cruise so far?"

"This view is breathtaking." He carefully gestured

with his wineglass, but he also meant her. She'd straightened her hair and it hung low over her chest. Light touches of pink makeup accented her eyes and lips, and he had to talk himself out of staring at her. "I can't believe you've never taken one of these cruises before."

"It's one of those things I always said I'd do but never got around to."

"I'm surprised you never went with your ex."

"We usually stuck to the same types of dates, like dinner and movies." Frowning, she wiped a smudge of lipstick off the rim of her wineglass. "I guess we grew comfortable doing the same-old, same-old."

"My *pappous* always says if you're comfortable, do something that makes you uncomfortable. That's the best way to grow."

She scrunched her nose. "Pappous?"

"Grandpa."

"Your grandpa sounds like a wise man."

Ethan nodded. Right after he and Raechel got married, Pappous had always approved of Dad's decisions, like signing the merger contract with Raechel's family. The merger provided both fishing companies with a wider variety of seafood, expanding their markets and increasing revenue. If only all of Ethan's decisions had been as wise as Dad's, then maybe the family business wouldn't be in jeopardy.

The wind picked up, sending stray strands dancing in

front of Amanda's face. She turned away from the wind, toward Ethan. "I've been meaning to ask you something, and I hope you don't think I'm prying."

He swirled the red wine around in his glass and took a drink. "Ask away."

"The first night we met, you mentioned not wanting to go back to Greece yet. How come?"

Ethan stiffened. If Amanda knew the truth, she wouldn't think very highly of him. Better to stick with the safe answer. "I don't want to leave before my training is done. The other doctors at the clinic I work for in Greece are counting on me to teach them everything I've learned here."

"Is there more to it than that? Something you're hiding from in Greece besides your nosy relatives?" She lifted her chin, staring directly into his eyes as she waited for an answer.

Ethan scratched the back of his head. He couldn't tell her the whole truth, but he could tell her part of it. He debated which part he'd share, while her unwavering gaze continued to linger. "My parents are mad at me because I got divorced. My ex-wife and her family are good family friends of ours, and they adore her."

"Oh. That's not what I was expecting." Amanda glanced down at her boots before meeting his gaze again. "How long ago did you get divorced?"

"Four years ago." Ethan cleared his throat. "My

parents have barely spoken to me since the divorce went through."

"Wow, that's awful."

"They are traditional people. None of our close relatives have ever been divorced. In their minds, I didn't try hard enough."

She studied his face as if she could see the torment hiding within. "I'm sure it was hard on you too."

"Yeah. My ex is the one who initiated it, but I didn't argue with her when she told me that's what she wanted." Ethan shrugged, trying not to make a big deal out of the situation.

Amanda nodded, not pressing him for more.

Good. His failed marriage still brought an ache to his chest—too many arguments, followed by too many bad choices and unfortunate circumstances.

"I can't imagine going through a divorce. Breakups are hard enough as it is."

"Have you talked to Tyler since my adjustment?"

Amanda uncrossed her ankles and turned to face the river. "I saw him last week. It was really awkward, but it's not like I can get away from him. We're on the Maple Valley Community Committee together."

"What's a community committee?"

"It's a group of Maple Valley citizens who help organize events. When I was younger, my mom used to be the president."

"Any events coming up?"

Amanda nodded. "The pumpkin patch is next weekend. After that, we have a health fair and a haunted house. And the last fall event is our annual festival."

"That sounds fun."

"It is … Well, it was. Now, it's just hard to be around Tyler."

"I get it. Even when I was around, my parents would still spend a lot of time with my ex-wife and her family. They still do. They own a fishing company together and my ex-wife works there." The moment he spoke, he wanted to take it back. So much for not talking about Raechel anymore. But there was something about Amanda that compelled him to open up.

"I bet you're glad to work somewhere else besides a family business, then."

"My parents weren't too thrilled at first. As the only boy in the family, my dad always hoped I'd take over the business one day. But after Sophia went into remission, I knew I wanted to be an oncologist one day. My parents understand my choice, but they're still disappointed."

"Do you think they'll come around eventually?"

"Come around?"

"Get over it."

Ethan swirled the wine in his glass. "I hope so. My ex-wife just got remarried, so at the very least, my parents can stop wishing we'll get back together."

"Does it bother you that she got remarried?"

"No. I love Raechel, but I'm not in love with her, not like I was."

Amanda nudged her shoulder against his. "I'm sure dating so many other women has helped too."

He arched an eyebrow. "I can't catch a break with you, can I?"

Laughing, she pointed a finger at him. "Ah, you didn't deny what I said."

Ethan shook his head. "So this community committee … Why don't you take a break from it this year? Save yourself the misery of seeing your ex."

Amanda narrowed her eyes, a slight smile tugging at her lips. "You're very good at deflecting the topic of conversation. But I'll answer your question anyway. I refuse to quit something I enjoy just because of Tyler. Even though it's hard to be around him, you never know: maybe he has a good reason for wanting a break."

For some inexplicable reason, a pang of jealousy struck his chest. "Are you saying you'd take him back?"

"He's a great guy. He's very driven, confident, and smart."

Ethan nodded, noticing she hadn't mentioned fun, compassionate, and loyal—qualities that Amanda deserved to have in a boyfriend.

"Tyler's hesitant to settle down and get married. His parents got divorced when he was young. He doesn't want to make the same mistakes they did."

Ethan took a drink of wine. He could see why Amanda would have compassion for Tyler, but the guy seemed like a coward to Ethan. "If you ask me, it sounds like a cop-out. When you know, you know."

"Oh yeah?" She gave him a doubtful look. "Did you think your wife was *the one*, then?"

"No, I don't believe in *the one*."

"Why not?"

"There are many possible people who could be right for you. The person you marry is more about finding the right someone at the right place and the right time."

"Is this a Greek philosophy?" Amanda asked.

"No, it's mine."

"Ah."

Silence settled between them as the sun disappeared below the horizon and stars appeared in the darkening sky. An oldies tune floated up from the first deck.

Ethan turned around to face the inside of the boat. Couples moved to the middle of the deck, dancing as the vocalist sang, "Sittin' on the dock of the bay …" Leaning his back against the railing, he sent Amanda a teasing look. "If you hadn't given me the third degree tonight, I might have asked you to dance."

She gave him a playful shove. "You're unbelievable, you know that, right?"

"I prefer to think of myself as incorrigible," he said.

Amanda giggled, the sound igniting warmth deep inside his chest. "Incorrigible? Did you really just use that word?"

"No matter what I say, I can never win with you." Ethan nudged her in the side, enjoying the flirtatious banter far too much. He'd never flirted like this with Raechel. He'd known her for so long before they got married that they'd never dated for the purpose of getting to know one another.

"What are you doing next weekend?" Amanda asked.

"Why? What do you have in mind?"

"Do you want to go to the pumpkin patch with me?"

He ran a hand over his jaw. Of course he did. But he didn't want to toy with her heart. "The thing is … I don't want to give you the wrong impression."

She tucked a strand of hair behind her ear.

"Like I said earlier, my parents are traditional people. They are proud of our Greek heritage and they expect my siblings and me to marry Greek." He turned toward her completely. "And even if they didn't mind, I'm not looking for anything serious right now."

Her eyebrows pinched together before her expression softened. "I don't want that either. I'm not over Tyler and I hope we'll get back together." She put her hand on his forearm. "I had fun with you tonight. As long as we're honest about not wanting more, why not hang out again?"

"I agree." He grinned. It was a win-win for everyone. Amanda knew they couldn't date and she still wanted to hang out. Plus, Ray had said that Ethan would be the perfect distraction for Amanda, but after tonight, he realized it would work both ways. Amanda would be a great diversion from all the problems awaiting him in Greece.

Chapter 9

IN THE HOSPITAL cafeteria, Amanda nibbled on a homemade protein bar. Dad was upstairs doing his next round of chemo and watching *Rudy*. She'd watched the movie so many times she knew almost every word.

Plus, she needed a quieter place to call some of her patients. Many of them were due in the next couple of months and she needed to plan home visits, where she could sit down with women and educate them on birth options, labor, and the postpartum period. Knowing what to expect helped women mentally prepare for multiple situations that could occur.

"I'd like a turkey and cheese sandwich." Grace's voice carried through the quiet cafeteria.

Amanda looked up as Grace paid for her sandwich and scanned the cafeteria for a place to sit.

Their gazes met and a panicked look crossed Grace's face. She quickly recovered and slowly walked toward Amanda's table. "Hey. How are you doing?"

Warmth spread across Amanda's chest. Most people

asked how Dad was doing, which she appreciated, but Grace had asked how *she* was doing. As a social worker, Grace probably understood that cancer affected family members too. Amanda thought about giving a generic answer but chose to be honest instead. "I have ups and downs. Sometimes, I'm hopeful and other times it feels like I'm crawling into a dark hole that I can't get out of."

Grace fiddled with the wrapping on her sandwich. "I'm sure your emotions are all over the place. The important thing is to fully give in to whichever emotion you're feeling. No matter what happens to your dad, it will help you heal from this traumatic time."

Nodding, Amanda gave Grace an appreciative smile. "Do you want to sit?"

Grace bit her bottom lip. She glanced at the elevator but sat down, perching on the edge of her chair. She pulled a cell phone out of her pocket and set it on the table as if she were waiting for a call. "Ethan told me that you're skeptical of invasive treatment."

Amanda nodded. It didn't bother her that Grace had told Ethan about Mom's suicide, but Amanda had to wonder: what else did Ethan and Grace talk about?

Grace tore the wrapping off her sandwich and took a bite. "Are you concerned about chemo tearing down his immune system?"

"Yeah, but I'm also worried about the emotional side effects."

"Because of your mom." Grace didn't have to ask.

"Yeah."

"Your mom's depression was much different than your dad's lung cancer," Grace said in a quiet tone.

"Are they different?" Amanda picked up her protein bar without biting into it. "What if the treatment becomes too much to handle? What if chemo doesn't work and he loses the will to fight, or worse, he tries to take his own life before his cancer gets worse?"

Grace put her elbows on the table, holding the sandwich with both hands. "I don't see your dad getting to that point, not after losing your mom the way you did. I highly doubt he would do that to you and Caleb."

Amanda chewed on her thumbnail. "I wish I could talk to him about what he's going through, but every time I try, he acts like everything is fine. It drives me crazy."

"Sometimes, especially when parents get cancer, they still try to protect their children. Your dad is a very protective person, so he might be hiding some of his sickness or side effects from you. I'd suggest telling him it's okay to be honest with you."

"Okay." Her friend had always been good at giving advice. Even as a teenager, she'd listened and understood, wisely giving advice to their group of friends. "Thank you."

"Of course." Grace's cell phone vibrated on the table.

An image of the caller popped up on the screen—a boy in a T-ball uniform, holding a bat. Red blotches appeared on Grace's neck as she pressed *Accept Call* and shot out of her chair. She rushed away from the table as she spoke.

Amanda sat still, her back rigid. She stared at the spot on the table where the phone had been. Who was the boy? Something about him looked familiar, but she couldn't pinpoint what exactly.

Grace came back as quickly as she left. "Sorry, I had to take that call."

"It's okay." She purposely hadn't asked Grace any personal questions after their last encounter, but curiosity itched at her insides. "Who was that boy?"

Grace froze for a moment as if she couldn't decide what to do. She picked up her sandwich, and ketchup oozed out of the bun. "He's my son. His name is Liam."

A son. Grace had a son. She couldn't wrap her head around it, especially if … She had to know. "How old is he?"

"He's nine."

Grace had left Maple Valley ten years ago. Amanda slouched back against her chair. She pressed a hand against her abdomen, the missing puzzle pieces of Grace's disappearance finally coming together. "You moved away because you were pregnant."

Grace glanced down at her lap, the spots on her neck

growing darker. "Yes." The word came out slow as if it took every bit of effort to speak.

"Why didn't you tell me? We used to tell each other everything."

Grace didn't answer. Instead, she rewrapped her sandwich and stood.

Amanda resisted the urge to ask more questions. Who was Liam's dad? Liam didn't look like Caleb, but what if Grace had hidden a son from her brother all these years? "Wait. Don't go."

"I need to get back to work."

Amanda sighed. "Just so you know, I'm here for you. You can talk to me."

"No, I can't." Grace turned and strode out of the cafeteria. Her long braid swung across her slender back.

Amanda wanted to follow her. The part that remembered how close they'd been wanted to reach out and comfort Grace. But things were different now. They weren't best friends anymore.

She rubbed her temples, contemplating whether or not she should tell her brother, but what would she say? *Hi, Caleb. How are things in Iraq? By the way, is there a chance you got Grace pregnant?*

She should've paid more attention years ago to the subtle changes in Grace, like during their last sleepover. The night had been planned for a while, but Grace had arrived late and disheveled. She'd flinched from Amanda's hug and shrugged off any questions, claiming to be stressed about school. Amanda had been excited to just spend time with her friend who had been abnormally busy over the past few months. The sleepover was supposed to be a way for them to reconnect.

Instead, Grace kept excusing herself to go to the bathroom and she only picked at a slice of Hawaiian pizza, her favorite. They talked about the future: Amanda planned on going to a college close by, while Grace had been accepted at a college in Missouri.

After the conversation, Grace had seemed upset and fell asleep early, leaving Amanda confused. But she'd been caught up in her own thoughts about graduating from high school and starting college. She'd planned to question Grace later about her friend's strange behavior but there hadn't been a next time. A few days later, Grace was gone.

AMANDA RETIED THE baby blue scarf around her neck, glancing at Ethan out of the corner of her eye. It felt odd to be at Piper's Pumpkin Patch with him instead of Tyler, but after the River Boat Cruise, she had no doubt they'd have a good time together.

He wasn't bad to look at either. He seemed to pull off everything he wore: tattered jeans and a plaid shirt, a leather jacket when he rode his motorcycle—heck, he even looked good in hospital scrubs.

"What do you want to do first?" he asked.

"Let's see …" Tapping a finger against her lips, she eyed the crowded, hilly terrain. Near the entrance, families sat at picnic tables, nibbling on popcorn and sipping from steaming Styrofoam cups. Tall, large pine trees surrounded the edge of the clearing, except for a wide, man-made path at the edge of the woods. Two hayrack rides sat idling in the path as people hopped on to pick out pumpkins. A train rumbled along a small, circular track with parents following next to it, smiling as their toddlers clapped in delight. "Unfortunately, I think we're too old for the train."

Ethan gave her a playful glare. "Speak for yourself."

Several volunteers from the committee waved at Amanda, sending curious glances at her and Ethan. She'd have a lot of explaining to do at the next meeting. They'd probably spend the first half of the meeting pestering her with questions about Ethan.

Ignoring their looks, she pointed to a fenced-off area. "How about the corn cannon? That looks more age-appropriate for us."

He rubbed his palms together. "Oh yeah, let's do that."

A few minutes later, they stood in front of two guns loaded with corn. Ethan leaned back, pulling the corn container as far back as it could go.

She tried not to notice how his chest muscles bulged beneath his dark, long sleeve T-shirt and watched as Ethan let go of the corn container.

A cornstalk shot in the direction of the target—a wooden board with a small hole in the middle of a painted-on pumpkin. He missed the hole by a couple of inches. "*Gamóto.*"

"I have no idea what you just said, but don't be discouraged. I can't imagine anyone being good at this." She took the same position as Ethan had and took her first shot. The cornstalk sailed through the air, then swooshed directly into the hole. Her eyes widened. "No way."

Ethan crossed his arms. "No one's good at this, huh? Does Iowa have a corn shooting team I should know about?"

Amanda laughed. "No. It was probably a fluke."

"There's only one way to find out. Go again."

She felt Ethan's gaze on her as she shot off another cornstalk. The stalk looked like it might fall short, but the wind held it up, carrying it through the hole once again. She shot a fist in the air. "Yes!"

He dropped his chin to his chest. Dark strands of hair fell across his forehead.

"Don't be a sore loser." She put a hand under his chin, lifting it so he could see her smirking.

"Okay, okay. Good job." He pushed the hair out of his eyes and gave her a high-five as they walked toward the concession stand. "No more shooting corn. Let's grab something to eat. That made me hungry."

A high-five? Now it was her turn to sulk. Even if they weren't dating, he didn't have to treat her like one of his buddies. Ignoring the ache in her chest, she pretended to cough into her hand. "Sore loser."

"You'd better watch it; I'm a black belt in Tae Kwon Do."

She made a *tsk* noise. "Threats are taken very seriously in the US."

"In that case ..." He put a hand over his heart. "I'm sincerely sorry."

"I forgive you."

Stopping at the end of the long concession stand line, Ethan turned toward her, his expression serious. "How is your dad feeling today?"

Her lips drew into a thin line, all joking forgotten. As much as she enjoyed spending time with Ethan, chemo was also the reason Dad had been so sick the last couple of days. In her darkest moments, fear consumed her every thought. Would the chemotherapy work? Would he survive? And if he did, what long-term effects would the chemo produce? "He's thrown up a few times, and he's been in bed most of the day."

"I know it's terrible to watch him go through that,

but the chemo has to fight off all those bad cells, which includes killing the good ones too."

"Only time will tell, huh?" She kept her tone flat.

"I'm glad you're at home to take care of him."

Amanda nodded. "Me too." It didn't seem like Ethan was judging her for still living with her dad, but just in case, she felt compelled to clarify her plans. "I will move out of my dad's eventually. I mean, I do hope to get married and start a family one day."

Ethan dug his black and white checkered shoes into the grass. He stared up at the menu without responding.

Had she said something that upset him?

Standing behind the concession stand, Sandy smiled, displaying two rows of yellow teeth. She looked at Ethan, eyeing him up and down like a piece of chocolate from Candy Galore. "Haven't seen you in a while, handsome. My shop not good enough for your dates anymore?"

Ethan's naturally olive cheeks turned red, but he quickly recovered, patting his stomach. "I need to cut back. Every time I buy a bag of candy, it's gone by the next day. Apparently, I have no self-control."

Amanda bit her bottom lip. No self-control with sweets or women?

"What would you like to order?" Sandy asked.

Amanda reached for her billfold. "I'll have a bag of unbuttered popcorn."

Before she could pay, Ethan slid a twenty-dollar bill

across the counter. “And I’d like cotton candy.”

Sandy raised her thin, white eyebrows. “You two an item?”

“No,” Amanda said at the same time as Ethan. “We’re just …”

“Friends,” Ethan finished.

Amanda forced herself to smile at Sandy. Waving good-bye, she walked past the long line and slumped down at a wooden table. Why was she disappointed when she didn’t want anything out of this relationship either? It must be Dad’s diagnosis, heightening her emotions.

Ethan sat down next to her, opened his bag, and untwisted a strand of sugary-looking cotton. “This might sound weird, but as much as I hated my family’s nosiness, I’ll miss Maple Valley for that exact same reason. Somehow, when the people are nosy here, it’s endearing.”

Her chest swelled at Ethan’s sentiment. Tyler had never spoken that highly of Maple Valley. She’d visited Chicago several times with him, and while they were in the city, she could tell how much he missed it. But he’d never said so, and she hadn’t wanted to ask, afraid of what he’d say. “There is something special about this town. The people are always here for you. When my mom died, people brought over meals for months. They even planned a high school graduation party for Caleb and me, knowing my dad wouldn't be up to planning one for us."

"That says a lot about this place. I've never lived in a small town before now. I'm from Chora. If you've never heard of it, it's because most people think of it as Mykonos. The nightlife is legendary, so we have a lot of tourists. You get used to seeing many unfamiliar faces."

"A lot of tourists is probably better for your family's fishing company, though, isn't it?"

"Yeah, my ex-wife's cousin does boat tours of the sea and he promotes our seafood. That's one of the reasons my family's fishing company merged with my ex's. We had a lot of the local business, while her family focused on tourists, so the merger brought in a ton of business for both of our families. Now, we're one of the biggest fishing companies in the area." His voice was strained as he told her, but his eyes lit up as he pulled out his phone and showed her a picture of the coast and one of their fishing boats.

She peered at the screen. Tall, white buildings towered above a long, sandy beach. Sunlight shimmered on a big boat that floated above the crystal blue sea.

"Wow, it's beautiful." She winked. "Not quite like Maple Valley, but very pretty."

Ethan shook his head, slipping the phone back into his pocket. "What's your favorite part about living here, besides the people?"

"That's easy—this town has the best festivals. We have the Cajun Food Festival in the summer, but my favorite is the fall festival."

"I've never made it to the Maple Valley Fall Festival. I've always had to work a shift at the hospital. What do you do there?"

"We'll have stations set up all over Bishop's Farm right outside of town. We'll have a pie eating contest, bobbing for apples, a corn maze, face painting and a barn dance."

Ethan stripped off another strand of cotton candy, wrapping it in a ball before tossing it in his mouth. "Maybe I should take off this year."

"So you'll come?"

"How could I say no? You made it sound so compelling."

"Great." She smiled, rolling the popcorn bag closed. "Ready for the hayrack ride?"

"Yeah." Ethan threw their snacks away before they walked toward the edge of the woods. "I want to find the biggest, ugliest pumpkin there is."

She gave him a strange look. "Why?"

"Because no one else looks for the biggest, ugliest pumpkin, and I like to be different."

"Whatever floats your boat."

"Huh?"

Amanda laughed. "Whatever makes you happy."

He stopped near the hayrack ride and gave her his hand, helping her up into the truck.

What a gentleman. She held on to his hand a moment too long, enjoying the way her hand felt inside his. She pulled it back and settled into an open spot on the crowded truck bed.

He hopped up and sat down next to her, putting his arm across the railing of the truck. If he moved his arm any lower, it would be around her shoulders. Sitting this close, she caught the faint scent of his cologne—a mix of sandalwood, musk, and oakmoss. It distracted her for a moment and she thought about leaning in closer to him before she collected her wits. Not that long ago, she'd seen Emily Johnson nestling against Ethan's side at a booth in Candy Galore.

Amanda turned her head, the image of Ethan and Emily stinging more than she was willing to admit.

"Whatever floats your boat. I'll have to keep that one in mind," Ethan said more to himself than to her. "Idioms don't translate across cultures very well."

"I know. That's why it's funny to say them to you. You look cute when you're confused." Heat flamed beneath her cheeks. Did she really just say that out loud? Before she could feel too embarrassed, the truck came to a stop in front of a large hill scattered with pumpkins.

A few minutes later, they strolled across the hill, analyzing several big, ugly pumpkins.

"Do you see anything you like?" he asked.

"Not yet. I'm looking for a small, cute pumpkin."

"Cute?"

"I'll show you when I find it."

Ethan stopped in front of a pumpkin that reached at least a foot tall. It had a thick stem with green, wart-like bumps all over it.

Amanda wrinkled her nose. "How can you even carve a pumpkin like that?"

"I don't plan on carving on it." He glanced up from the pumpkin. "I'll let my little cousins draw on it."

"That's sweet of you." She smiled. "How are you going to carry a pumpkin that big?"

"Are you doubting my strength?" In one fluid movement, he lifted the pumpkin and rested it on his shoulder. The movement caused his T-shirt to lift, showcasing hard, lean abs.

Amanda licked her lips, imagining her fingers slowly running over his washboard abs, then … *Whoa.* Reality check. Her fingers weren't going anywhere near his bare skin. What was wrong with her today? She must be missing Tyler and it was affecting her feelings for Ethan. That had to be it.

She turned away from him to peer at the ground. A few feet away sat a little, round pumpkin with a thin, curved stem. She pointed at it. "That's the one. It's perfect."

"Oh. I see what you mean. Very cute." Sarcasm laced his tone.

She rolled her eyes. "Let's get back on the truck, so you can put your pumpkin down."

A bead of sweat trickled down his face. "I'm fine. I could hold this baby all day."

"Uh-huh, sure."

Smirking, she weaved through the large pine trees, the rumbling sound of the truck's engine growing closer. Jerry, one of the volunteers, lifted their pumpkins into the bed of the truck. A group of teenagers scooted over to make room for them. Once everyone was seated, the truck traveled across an uneven gravel path.

Ethan turned to look at her, their faces inches apart. "In Greece, we don't technically celebrate Halloween, in the strict sense of the word. We celebrate Apokries. It's a celebration in February that lasts three weeks, leading up to Lent. Everyone dresses up in costumes and fills the streets. It's a blast, especially the Grand Carnival Parade at the end."

"Wow, a three-week party. It sounds like a lot of fun." She sat up straighter. "You just gave me an idea. We could encourage everyone to wear costumes for the fall festival."

Ethan grinned. "I like it."

A smile spread across her face. Talking to Ethan had made her realize how closed off she'd been by living in

Maple Valley her entire life. The world was so much bigger, with many different cultures and customs that she had yet to explore.

She reached for the small pumpkin, holding it against her chest. "I'm really glad you're here."

"Me too." He winked at her.

Her heart raced. Even if Ethan had taken several women on dates to Candy Galore, he wasn't with any of them now. He was sitting next to her, winking at her. Not Emily. Not Jesse. Not Sierra. *Her.*

Amanda turned back toward him as he glanced down at her lips and looked up quickly, meeting her gaze. She swallowed hard. Was he thinking about kissing her? Did she want him to kiss her? Before she could think about it for too long, the truck drove over a big rock, causing them to bump heads.

Laughing, she leaned back and put a hand on her forehead. "Ugh, that hurt."

He rubbed his forehead and sent her a lopsided grin, making the cleft in his chin more pronounced. "Sorry about that."

Her lips parted. Was he sorry for bumping heads or sorry for almost kissing her? If that's what he'd been thinking about at all. Now that the moment was over, she was second-guessing herself. Ethan was probably used to kissing his dates and he'd had a fluke reaction, sitting so close to her. He hadn't actually wanted to kiss her.

But a small spike of fear raced through her heart. If he had kissed her, she would've kissed him back.

ETHAN FLIPPED THE kill switch on, turned the keys in the ignition, and pressed start. His motorcycle rumbled to life. He twisted the throttle, revving the engine in an attempt to drown out his conversation with Uncle Cameron.

You're making a mistake, his uncle had said after overhearing people talk about Ethan and Amanda going to the pumpkin patch together.

Uncle Cameron wasn't happy. He'd already warned Ethan about befriending patients and family members.

Ethan slowly drove out of the driveway, watching to make sure none of his cousins—who were playing tag in the backyard—ran in front of his motorcycle. Coast clear, he turned onto the street. He increased speed, heading toward downtown. A light breeze blew past, cooling his face. If only it would blow away the rest of his conversation with Uncle Cameron.

But it didn't. His uncle's warning lingered like the stench of an infected wound. His uncle said he was looking out for Ethan. *Ray could die and you and Amanda will both be deeply affected.*

Uncle Cameron's warning also stemmed from deeper, more personal reasons. Falling for Amanda would ruin Ethan's chances of reconciling with his parents.

Ethan had reassured his uncle there was nothing to worry about. He wasn't stupid. Case in point: he hadn't kissed her on the hayrack ride. Even without his uncle's warning, Ethan knew the consequences of making a move were far too great.

But that didn't mean he couldn't think about it: her face inches away from his, her naturally rosy cheeks, her lightly-freckled nose, and her glossy pink lips. It had looked as if she'd wanted him to kiss her too. The desire had been in her eyes. And at that moment, he'd had to use every ounce of willpower not to kiss her. If he could resist once, he could do it again.

A minute later, he stepped inside Val's Diner, his senses ignited by freshly brewed coffee, sweet syrup, and salty bacon. His stomach rumbled. He should go to Dill's Grocery after breakfast and stock up on food. But he didn't feel like cooking this morning, and Val's Diner was a much better alternative.

He squeezed through to the bar to order. Standing behind the bar, Valerie glanced up at him, a wide smile spreading across her face. "Hey Ethan! What'll it be this mornin'?"

"The usual."

"I figured, but it never hurts to ask." Valerie put a hand on her voluptuous hip. "You lookin' for Amanda

Meyers?"

"Uh, no." Heat crept up the back of his neck. "I mean, I didn't know she was here."

Valerie lowered her voice. "I saw the way you were looking at Amanda at the pumpkin patch." She smiled, seeming to sense his unease, and pointed to a booth by the front window. "She's right over there."

Ethan glanced in that direction. Amanda leaned back in the booth, looking at the woman across from her and laughing. The other woman spoke, her dark features animated as she gestured wildly with her hands. If he remembered correctly, her name was Kendall.

He made his way in their direction, overhearing Grace's name. Amanda had said it, and her friend's eyes widened. All three of them had probably grown up together.

Amanda picked up a big piece of pancake with her fork, dipped it in syrup, and took a bite. As he neared the table, she spotted him and her cheeks turned bright red. She covered her mouth with a napkin.

The other woman at the table turned to look at him. "We've never officially met. I'm Kendall."

"It's nice to meet you." He looked at Amanda, not bothering to hide his amusement as he eyed the pile of pancakes on her plate. "So, you are human. It's nice to see that even you eat bad food once in a while."

Amanda lowered her napkin and swallowed. "Moment of weakness."

"Do you want to join us?" Kendall asked.

You're making a mistake. Uncle Cameron's words came back all too quickly. Ethan shoved his hands inside his pockets, pushing his uncle's reasoning aside. His uncle didn't understand. Spending time with Amanda was refreshing. Like an unexpected spring rain that he didn't want to end.

He slid in next to Amanda, leaned back, and rested a bent leg over his other knee. "What are you up to today?"

"I'm trying to convince Kendall to take my yoga class for pregnant women."

A waitress wearing a *Pride and Prejudice* T-shirt brought Ethan a plate of biscuits and gravy. She looked at Amanda. "That class of yours was the best thing I ever did while I was pregnant. My butt's never looked so good." She smiled and turned toward Kendall. "But beware: you're gonna hurt in places you didn't even know you had."

"You're not supposed to tell anyone that before class starts or else they won't come," Amanda said.

"Oops." The waitress giggled as she walked away, swaying her hips from side to side.

Kendall laughed. "I'm totally reconsidering now."

"Dang it." Amanda snapped her fingers, pretending to be angry until someone caught her eye. She sat up straighter and ran a hand through her curls.

Tyler strolled over to the booth, clutching a to-go cup with *chai* written in sloppy letters. A pinched expression flashed across his clean-shaven face as his gaze flitted to Ethan, but Tyler recovered quickly and looked at Amanda. "I was hoping you'd be here."

"Oh?" Amanda folded her napkin, pressing along the crease with her thumb.

Tyler took a sip of his chai. "I wanted to talk to you about your dad's fundraiser. Have you thought of a location yet?"

Amanda shook her head. "Kendall and I made a list of possible places, but I haven't decided yet. Do you have any ideas?"

Ethan swallowed a bite of his biscuit. Tyler and Amanda were planning a fundraiser for Ray *together*? For some inexplicable reason, a sour taste filled his mouth.

"I've put a lot of thought into this." Tyler pushed back his shoulders. "I think the football stadium would be the perfect place. We could do it during a game, so everybody would already be there."

Amanda looked up at him, her eyes lighting with excitement. "I love that idea."

"Great. I'll work out more details over the weekend." Tyler beamed. "Well, I need to get going. I'm headed to Chicago." His gaze flickered to Ethan again. "Have a good one." The glowering look on his face said anything but.

Ethan furrowed his eyebrows. Tyler was either possessive or he still loved Amanda.

Disgust flickered through Ethan. It seemed like Tyler was just toying with Amanda's emotions. Why was it so hard for Tyler to be sure he wanted to be with her?

Amanda deserved better. She deserved a man who knew how lucky he was to have her.

Chapter 10

AMANDA OPENED THE linen closet and reached for a cloth and an all-natural cleaning spray. Walking into Dad's bedroom, she turned on the old radio next to his bed. Country music filled the room as she sprayed the cloth and wiped the top of the nightstand. It didn't look dusty at all—she'd cleaned his room less than a week ago—but ever since his diagnosis, she'd made an effort to clean more often, especially on days when he went to work at the Canine Palace.

It was easier to clean while he was gone, but deep down she knew there was more to it than that. She was worried about him working too many hours. Part-time seemed like too much. She'd suggested he stop working until he was done with chemo, but he'd waved his hand in nonchalance, telling her that he needed a bit of normalcy to keep him sane.

She understood his reasoning, but she shuddered at the thought of all those people and dogs in his store, touching products and spreading germs. Flu season was almost here and his immune system might not be strong enough to handle it.

Amanda walked to the TV stand across from the bed. She sprayed the cloth, kneeled down in front of the stand, and scrubbed the polished wood until it shined. Every surface of the house felt like a potential threat to him, unseen bacteria in every crevice.

She cleaned the house for the next two hours, until she finally felt satisfied. She needed to hop in the shower and get ready for tonight. Ethan had asked her if she wanted to go to the haunted house with him.

Imagining Ethan's smile made the tension in her shoulders loosen slightly. She hadn't expected the chemistry between them to be so magnetic. She hadn't expected to have so much fun with him. Being with Ethan made her giddy in a way that she hadn't felt in a long time.

And yet, Ethan had made it very clear that they couldn't date. Part of her respected him for being honest, but she also felt disappointed. What made her different from all those other women he'd gone on dates with over the last few years? Had he told them the same thing? Was it because he was treating her dad?

Whatever Ethan's reasons were, it was probably for the best. She still had Tyler to consider. His idea to hold the fundraiser at the football stadium meant so much to her. But she couldn't help wondering why he felt so compelled to help. He said he cared about her; did that mean he was still in love with her?

If so, would he be ready to settle down and have a family soon? The idea of Tyler taking his time to decide didn't bother her as much as it once had. And yet, if he wanted to work things out, she would give him another chance. She owed it to their relationship to see it through.

STEPPING INTO THE darkness, Amanda clutched Ethan's hand. Loud screaming echoed down the foggy corridor. Adrenaline pumped through her veins as they cautiously walked farther inside the haunted house.

Suddenly, a mummy jumped out from the wall, wailing and moving his arms up and down.

Amanda screamed. "Run!"

Ethan pulled her past the mummy and into another hallway. Creepy, raggedy dolls surrounded them on both sides of the walls. She closed her eyes, following Ethan blindly.

Ethan moved close to her ear, his breath tickling her neck. "You're not scared, are you?"

She opened her eyes and shrugged. "No, of course not. I'm just acting scared to make you feel manlier."

"You're so thoughtful."

A tall, large man with a chainsaw ran down the hallway toward them. The closer he got, the louder the roar of his chainsaw grew.

Amanda yelped and jumped between Ethan and the wall farthest from the man. Instinctively, she put a hand on his arm, noticing the hard muscles beneath her palm. She was really starting to get the whole 'Greek god' nickname. Clearly, she spent too much time with Kendall.

"Yeah, you're not scared at all." Ethan chuckled.

She dropped her hand and jabbed him in the ribs. "Don't laugh at me."

But Ethan continued to laugh as they passed a group of ghosts, a witch who pretended to cast a spell on them, and a cackling clown. Amanda made an effort to keep her hands to herself, but they walked side by side, their shoulders brushing against one another. Her nerve endings tickled each time it happened.

Several minutes later, they ran out of the haunted house and stopped in the lobby of the old mansion. Amanda bent over, setting her hands on her knees. "Now I remember why I usually sign up to *plan* the haunted house. Then I know what's coming and it isn't as scary."

"Glad you realized it after we did the haunted house."

"Yeah, except I probably won't sleep tonight."

"Let's do something else, then."

She put a finger to her lips in thought as they walked out of the mansion into the parking lot. "I have an idea."

"Care to enlighten me?"

"No. I'll drive us there."

Ethan pointed to himself, then to her. "You want *me* to get into a car with *you*?"

She put her hands on her hips and narrowed her eyes. "I already told you I'm a good driver."

"How about I drive?" He gestured to his motorcycle, parked near the building. "You can tell me how to get wherever we're going."

Her chest rose and fell. "I don't know."

Ethan held out his hand, palm up. "Oh, come on. If you've never been on a motorcycle before, it'll be a real thrill."

Fear and excitement sent a rush of adrenaline through her veins. "All right. I'm in," she said, following Ethan to his bike.

Ethan retrieved a second helmet, slid it over her head, and gently buckled the strap beneath her chin. As the buckle snapped, he winked at her. "It looks good on you."

He probably said that to all the women who rode with him, but that didn't stop her from feeling giddy and light-headed.

"Ready?"

Nodding, Amanda followed Ethan's lead and swung

her leg over the bike in a straddle position. She wrapped her arms around his waist as he revved up the engine and put on his own helmet. She bit back a grin. *This was seriously happening.*

"Where should I go?" he asked over the roar of the engine.

She leaned forward, resting her chin on his shoulder to give him directions. At the end, she said, "You'll know you're in the right place when you see a lot of lights."

"Okay." He drove out of the parking lot, heading toward the highway.

The wind picked up, whipping past them. In the distance, the sun dipped below the horizon, coloring the sky in shades of deep purple and blue with streaks of yellow. They drove past farms, the faint scents of horses and cows drifting by them, only to be replaced by fresh air moments later.

She let out an exhilarated giggle. She felt like Rose, standing on the bow of the Titanic, welcoming a loss of control and a sense of freedom like she'd never felt before. Maybe when Ethan left, she'd buy a bike of her own.

A pinch of disappointment squeezed inside her chest. She didn't want to think about Ethan moving away.

He decreased speed and exited the highway. A mile away stood a large building illuminated with bright lights. The grounds around the building had multicolored lights, running in different directions. A plane took off, soaring above their heads. "Now where?"

"That way." She pointed to a dark path off the main road. It had been years since she'd been here, but she found the spot easily, nestled between two oak trees that had lost half of their leaves. "Stop here."

Ethan helped her off the bike and removed her helmet. "This is cool. How did you find this spot?"

"My brother and I found it when we were off-roading in his Jeep." She sat down in the grassy area, extending her legs. "The planes fascinated Caleb, and I loved thinking about all the people. I always wondered where they were going or what they were planning to do."

Ethan sat down next to her and rested his arms behind him, leaning back in a comfortable position. "Sounds to me like you need to go on a trip."

She nodded. It hadn't been too long ago that she and Tyler were supposed to go to Florida together. So much had happened since then. It was weird to think that a lot of it wouldn't have happened if she'd gone on that trip.

"You should go somewhere far away, somewhere you've never been before," Ethan said.

"I haven't traveled a lot. When I was a kid, my family went to Mount Rushmore, Yellowstone Park, and Disney World. But as we got older and my mom's depression grew worse, we stopped traveling." Amanda frowned. "And I won't be leaving for that kind of trip anytime soon. Not while my dad is sick."

"When he gets better, you should consider it." Ethan nudged her with his shoulder. "Of course, I'd recommend Greece."

"Shocker. What would you suggest I do?"

"You could go sailing, or see the Acropolis. The Mythological Tour is cool, too. There's also a private tour of gourmet food. You walk around and try samples. I think you'd enjoy it."

Another plane took off overhead. She listened to the calming rumble of the jets as she pictured herself traveling. She wouldn't go alone. What would be the fun in that? Maybe she would take Kendall once her friend felt comfortable leaving her baby.

But when Amanda closed her eyes and imagined going to Greece, she saw Ethan with her, walking hand in hand on the beach. Surprised, she opened her eyes, not willing to let her imagination get out of control. They could never be together.

Leaning forward, Ethan turned toward her. "Is your heart rate back to normal yet after the haunted house and bike ride?"

His question reminded her of Kendall's most recent appointment a few days ago. It had taken longer than normal to find the baby's heart rate, scaring both Amanda and Kendall.

Ethan gave her a concerned look.

"Sorry, I was thinking about Kendall. I've had a hard time finding her baby's heartbeat during her check-up appointments. It always makes her worried. She's had three miscarriages."

Ethan stiffened. "That would be scary," he said in a somber tone. He looked away from her and picked up a leaf off the ground, twisting the stem between his thumb and pointer finger.

"What's wrong?"

"Nothing."

"I don't believe you," she said quietly.

He expelled a deep breath. "My ex-wife and I had a hard time getting pregnant."

"Oh no." Her chest constricted. It hurt to hear when any couple had a hard time conceiving, especially when some parents didn't want children or weren't stable enough to have them.

"After two years of trying, Raechel discovered she had endometriosis. So we tried IVF." Ethan's voice was low and husky. "It worked. We got pregnant, but …" He dropped the leaf, watching it fall to the ground. "We lost the baby shortly after."

Amanda moved closer to Ethan. She put her hand over his and entwined their fingers. "That must have been devastating."

Ethan met her gaze. The lights from the airport reflected off his face, illuminating the depth of pain in his eyes. "It was. We were both hurting and I wanted to be there for Raechel, to support her, but she blamed me."

"Why would it be your fault?"

He was silent for a moment, as if he couldn't decide how to answer. "One night we got into a bad fight about our finances. It was before we knew she was pregnant, and I left. We needed some time apart to cool down. So I stayed at my oldest sister's for a couple of weeks." He ran a hand over his face. "Raechel discovered she was pregnant while I was gone, but she didn't tell me."

He glanced up at the sky, a faraway look clouding his eyes. "When she called and asked me to come over, I thought she wanted to reconcile. But she told me she'd lost our baby and it was my fault because I'd left and stressed her out."

"You know it's not your fault, though, right? Sometimes, miscarriages just happen and there's no way to prove what caused it."

"I know. It's still hard, though. When I look at other people's kids, I wonder what my baby would've looked like. Was it a boy or a girl? What would his or her personality have been like?"

Amanda rested her head on his shoulder. A glimmer of understanding pulsed through her heart. After such a loss, Ethan had probably wanted a break from any serious relationship. Maybe he wasn't a ladies man, after all; he just needed time to heal. "I can't believe your parents are barely speaking to you knowing you went through such a tough time."

"They don't know about the infertility issues or the miscarriage. No one in my family knows."

Amanda lifted her head off his shoulder. "Why haven't you told them?"

"For Raechel's sake. Her parents have pressured her for grandchildren for years. She doesn't want anyone to know, and I don't want to make her feel worse than she already does. It's better if I wait until she's ready to tell our families. Hopefully, she'll tell them one day."

Amanda stared at him with a newfound admiration. Ethan was the kind of guy who would still respect his ex-wife even after she blamed him for something that was out of his control. "You're an amazing man, and one day, you'll be a great dad."

"I'm not sure I want to get married again or have kids for that matter."

She leaned forward so she could look him straight in the eye. "Why not?"

Ethan shrugged. "It's not that I don't want kids, it's just … Raechel and I made each other miserable. I don't know if I want to get married and have the same thing happen again."

Amanda scowled. "That's ridiculous. Don't be so bitter that it prevents you from having the family you've always wanted."

"I should've known you'd argue with me on this." He shook his head, sending her a small smile. "Do you want kids?"

Once again, Ethan had diverted the attention from him to her. But she wouldn't point it out this time. She didn't want to argue with him; she just wanted him to see that he had other options. "I'd love to have a big family. Three or four kids, at least."

"If you're half as good at motherhood as you are at being a daughter, you'll be great."

A flow of contentment traveled through her chest. Tyler had never given her a compliment like that. Somehow, even though she'd only met Ethan a couple of months ago, he knew just what to say to make her feel good. Really good.

Don't get too attached, she reminded herself. In a couple of months, Ethan would live halfway across the world. Even if that made her sad, she had no chance of getting him to stay.

ETHAN WHEELED A cart down the hallway of the oncology unit. His laptop rattled against the metal cart. Uncle Cameron and several other staff members from the oncology department walked in front of him and stopped in front of each patient's open door for morning rounds. Some patients didn't come to the door to hear what Ethan's team had to say about their condition and treatment plan, while others asked every question they could possibly think of.

This morning it was hard to focus on any patient with Amanda on his mind.

Last night had been amazing. At the haunted house, she'd wrapped her arm around his like a vise grip. She was a strong, independent woman, not the type to lean on others, but she'd clutched his arm as if the haunted house volunteers were really out to get them. He'd enjoyed protecting her.

More importantly, he'd never opened up to anyone about losing his baby, and even though Amanda had never experienced a miscarriage, she seemed to understand the hurt it still caused him and the strain it had put on his previous marriage. Surely, she'd met patients who had gone through similar situations.

After seeing her reaction, he'd considered opening up about everything—the entire reason he and Raechel had divorced, but he'd decided not to. The truth would stretch the limits of Amanda's compassion and she'd no doubt end things between them. Something he wouldn't chance. For the first time since his divorce, he felt hopeful.

Ethan and his team neared the end of the hallway

and stopped in front of the last patient's room. He pulled up Lydia's file on his computer screen. Over the weekend, she'd been admitted for inpatient chemo.

She shuffled to the doorway in her slippers and robe and leaned against the doorway. "Morning."

"Good morning, Lydia." Ethan cleared his throat. If only he had better news for her. "Unfortunately, chemo isn't making a difference in the size of the tumor."

Lydia undid the straps around the waist of her robe and tied them in a tight knot. "What's the next treatment option, then?"

Ethan squared his shoulders. He needed to sound calm and confident to ease any worries Lydia might have. "I'd like to try radiation, and I'd like you to start as soon as possible."

The radiation oncologist typed notes into her laptop. "I'll ask my receptionist to put it on my schedule."

"Okay." Lydia lifted her chin, but her bottom lip quivered. "I'll do whatever it takes."

A lump formed in his throat. "I'll be back later to check on you, all right?"

She turned around and ambled back into her room.

He stood still for a moment, staring at the shiny floor as her shadow slowly disappeared. Defeat settled over him like a looming fog. Radiation would only give her a few more months at the very most, but it wouldn't save her life. He scrubbed a hand over his face, wishing there was more he could do for her.

Footsteps approached down the hallway, and he looked up to see Grace walking toward him. "Did you just talk to Lydia?" she asked.

"Yeah."

"Good. I'm glad she's up. I thought I'd go in to talk to her, try to cheer her up if she needs it." Grace shifted her weight from one foot to the other. "Are you okay? You look tired."

"I didn't get much sleep last night. I was up late. Amanda took me to the airport to watch planes take off."

"Oh." Grace tucked a strand of hair behind her ear. "I didn't realize the two of you were hanging out."

"Yeah. She's great."

Her eyes widened. "You like Amanda, don't you?"

"I, uh …" Ethan glanced down the hallway, checking to make sure his uncle wasn't nearby.

"She must've made quite the impression on you, already."

"Since when did you get so nosy?" Biting back a grin, Ethan nudged her with his elbow.

Grace flinched and stepped away, putting space between them.

"Sorry." His eyebrows furrowed together. "I didn't mean to scare you."

"It's okay. I'm just jumpy." She turned and moved closer to Lydia's room, then turned around to face him.

"I hope you don't take this the wrong way, but you're quite the charmer around here. It's never bothered me before, but if you're hanging out with Amanda, you'd better not break her heart."

His eyebrows rose. Grace wasn't usually so blunt. She must still care deeply about Amanda.

And if he was being honest with himself, he was starting to care about Amanda too. In fact, Grace didn't need to worry. If he spent much more time with Amanda, it might be *his* heart in the danger zone.

❦

AMANDA STOOD IN front of the community committee with Tyler. At the last meeting, he'd asked for a small group of volunteers to organize Dad's fundraiser, but everyone wanted to help. Hopefully, they would raise a lot of money. The medical bills were starting to come in, piling up on the kitchen table.

Tyler held his cell phone in front of him, taking notes. "Sandy, how are the T-shirts coming along?"

"I ordered them last week. They are black and orange with a Tiger paw on the breast pocket and *Team Meyers* written on the back."

"Great." Tyler smiled. "Kendall, what about marketing?"

Kendall swallowed the last bite of a white-powdered

donut, wiping her lips with a napkin. "I've created an event on social media and invited everyone in Maple Valley. I've also posted on every social media account I have. Plus, I made paper invites and handed them out to every store."

Tyler gave her a thumbs-up and turned toward Amanda. "I have plenty of volunteers signed up for the concession stand. I had to turn people away. We'll have some extra hands just in case it gets busier than normal."

Her throat thickened, fighting back a mixture of emotions. "Thank you."

Jason clapped his hands and waltzed to the front of the room. "Is that everything you need, Amanda?"

She shook her head. "Actually, I have one other idea I wanted to mention. It's for the fall festival. Since it's so close to Halloween, what if we asked everyone to dress up in Halloween costumes?"

For a moment, the room went silent.

Kendall leaned forward, her protruding belly pushing up against the table. "I love it."

Sandy picked at loose strands of white hair. "We've never done that before. I don't think we should make such a big change."

Mark nodded. "If it's not broken, don't fix it."

Kendall reached for a chocolate donut. "I'm sure kids would enjoy dressing up."

Jason shrugged. "Maybe it's something we could

consider next year."

"Okay." Sighing, Amanda sat down. In other words, he didn't want to talk about it anymore. Sometimes, the people in this town could be so closed-minded.

"I'd like to thank everyone who helped with the health fair," Jason said. "We had a fabulous turnout, and thanks to Tyler, we even had visitors from Chicago show up."

Amanda ran her tongue over her teeth. She'd been shocked to see Tyler's parents at the health fair. He hadn't told her they were coming. His parents had tried to talk to her like everything was normal between them, but they had looked at her differently, like they felt sorry for her. It could be because of Dad, but she had a gut feeling there was more to it than that. Tyler had probably told them why he'd wanted a break.

As soon as Jason concluded the meeting, she beelined for the door. She needed space away from Tyler.

"Wait." Tyler stepped in sync next to her as they walked out to the parking lot. "I need to ask you something."

Amanda adjusted the purse strap on her shoulder. So much for space. "What is it?"

Committee members filed out, sending them curious glances. He moved closer to her, lowering his voice. "I saw the way you looked at Ethan at Val's Diner. I'm surprised you're falling for him."

She crossed her arms, surprised he'd noticed, but it wasn't any of Tyler's business. "That wasn't a question."

"Why would you date someone who is only here for two more months?"

"We aren't dating, and how do you know he plans on moving back?"

"Don't get mad at me, but I've asked around. It sounds like the guy is only here on a visa." Tyler shoved his hands inside the pockets of his fleece. "You love Maple Valley. What would you do if he asked you to move to Greece?"

Amanda made a *hmpf* noise. Tyler had no right to be jealous. "You're getting a little ahead of yourself. I don't plan on moving anywhere. I love it here."

A look of disappointment flickered in his eyes.

She wrinkled her nose. Why would he be disappointed about that? Shouldn't he be relieved? None of this made sense.

He rocked back on his heels, keeping his tone casual. "So, you'd never move away?"

"Why does it matter?"

Tyler stepped closer and put his hands on her shoulders. "I'm worried about you. We broke up, then your dad got diagnosed with cancer, and now you're seeing someone else. It seems unlike you to be so reckless."

"Reckless?"

"Ethan's not the kind of guy you should be serious

with."

She crossed her arms. "And you are?"

"Well, yeah."

"I *was* serious about you, until you wanted a break."

He moved his hands to her waist and pulled her against him, pressing his lips against hers. The kiss was soft and slow, the kind of kiss after years of dating that brought comfort and warmth. She closed her eyes, waiting for her old feelings to resurrect.

But beneath closed lids, an image formed. It wasn't of Tyler and her. She wished she were kissing Ethan. The thought was enough to break the kiss. She put her hands on Tyler's chest and gently pushed him away. Anger simmered to the surface. How dare he think he could kiss her! "What are you doing?"

Tyler frowned, his features a mix of longing and sadness.

"Don't kiss me like that again, unless you decide you want to get back together. And then, only then, will I consider kissing you back." She turned and strode down the sidewalk, heading toward the Canine Palace to check on Dad. And to put more space between her and Tyler.

Chapter 11

ETHAN SLID THE results of Ray's blood work and most recent PET scan across his desk. The results detailed the changes in Ray's cancer since treatment began.

Sitting across from his desk, Ray squeezed Amanda's hand and leaned forward. His once rosy cheeks were gray and his cheekbones more prominent. He still had some of his original thick, gray hair, but it was falling out.

Ethan's gaze moved from Ray to Amanda. Time to give them the news.

Amanda adjusted in her chair, her gaze flitting from Ethan to the floor to Ethan again.

Sensing her nerves, he gave her a reassuring smile. "The chemo is working. Not as many hot spots showed up on the scan—about fifty percent less, in fact."

A sliver of hope lit in Amanda's big, beautiful eyes.

Ethan grinned and his chest filled with warmth. When he'd first read Ray's test results, he'd pumped his fist in the air. He'd never been more excited to share test results with a patient.

Ray noticeably swallowed. "You're sure?"

Ethan nodded. "Now that we know it's working, we'll stick to the original protocol to make sure it's all gone."

Ray slapped Ethan's desk with fervor. "This calls for a celebration. Why don't you come over for dinner tonight?"

"I'd love that." Ethan walked around his desk and shook Ray's hand. "I'll bring dinner, so neither of you has to cook."

Ray pulled him into a hug. "Thanks for everything."

"My pleasure." Ethan's voice was muffled against Ray's shoulder.

As they stepped out of their embrace, Amanda stepped closer and gave him an uncertain look. "I'm glad chemo is making a difference, but positive results at this point don't necessarily equate to remission, right?"

"Right," he said slowly. He should have known that even when things were going well that Amanda would still question chemotherapy. And yet, somehow he found her blunt honesty attractive. He never had to second-guess her.

Not like he'd done with Raechel. Throughout their marriage, Raechel had manipulated many situations. He'd noticed, but ignored them, trying to see the best in her. Until he couldn't any longer. Not after the night she'd come home from work and told him what she'd done.

After reassuring Amanda that the treatment results were encouraging and that he would see her tonight, he said good-bye and headed to Lydia's room. Her resilience in the face of such devastating news amazed him. She was determined to grasp on tight to whatever time she had left.

Four hours later, Ethan set a bowl of Caesar salad, a homemade pizza, and breadsticks on the table. He'd made an American meal for Ray and Amanda since Amanda had cooked a Greek dinner for him. "Where's your dad?"

"He's still sleeping. I tried to get him up an hour ago, but he suggested we eat without him. I'm surprised. He never misses an opportunity to eat. I think he's really tired."

Ethan couldn't help feeling a bit relieved that he could spend the night alone with Amanda. He felt a little guilty—Ray was the reason they were celebrating, but then Amanda bent over to put the pizza in the oven. Heat pooled low below his waist as he watched her leggings stretch tightly around her waist and thighs.

Amanda straightened, turned around, and caught his gaze.

He ran a hand through his hair. *Caught red-handed.* He reached for two bowls and filled them with salad.

"I, uh, I thought we could eat dinner outside," Amanda said. "We won't have many more warm nights like this."

"I like your thinking."

"The oven will ding when the pizza is ready, so we can go out now. Would you mind grabbing our drinks? We have sparkling water, coconut water, and almond milk."

He grabbed two sparkling waters and headed out the door behind her. A warm fall breeze blew across the deck. Sitting down, he bent his leg and rested it over the other.

Amanda sat down across from him, taking a small bite of her salad. "All my dad wants to do lately is sleep. It's so unlike him."

"Sophia slept a lot, too. She would even fall asleep in the middle of dinner."

"Your sister was so young when she had cancer. Is she still affected in any way now?"

"No. She goes in for routine checkups, but other than that she's fine." He swept a hand over the stubble on his face. "Even back then, she never let it get to her. My parents hired a tutor and she kept up with her studies. She had a positive attitude most of the time. Except when her face got puffy and she lost her hair."

"For a young girl, I can't imagine being bald."

"Sophia bought a wig soon after she shaved her head.

The wig looked real. But the worst part was when her hair grew back and made her head itchy."

"That must have been hard for you, too. How old were you?"

"I was thirteen."

"That's young. I'm an adult and I still have a hard time watching my dad go through it." Her voice sounded strained.

Ethan reached for her hand, slowly caressing his thumb across her palm. "I understand."

Amanda noticeably swallowed and slid her hand out of his.

Was she upset that he'd touched her? He shifted in his chair and cleared his throat.

"Sorry, it's not you." She set her fork down and leaned against the back of her chair. "It's Tyler."

His gut hardened. "What about Tyler?"

"He kissed me."

Ethan gritted his teeth. Every muscle in his body tensed at once, but he had no right to say anything.

"I really thought I wanted to get back together with him, but after he kissed me, I'm not so sure."

"Why not?"

"Partly because he shouldn't have kissed me. He's the one who wanted a break." She met Ethan's gaze and bit the side of her bottom lip.

An unbearably long silence followed where he

couldn't tear his eyes away from her partly opened mouth.

Finally, she blurted out, "But mostly because I wished I were kissing you."

"Oh." The air between them suddenly grew electric. He wanted to pull her onto his lap and kiss her in a way that would make her never want to go back to her ex.

"We said we would be honest. I don't expect anything from telling you. The last thing I want is to ruin things with your family."

"I appreciate that." His voice sounded husky and low. He stood up quickly. "I'll go check on the pizza."

Inside, he gripped the kitchen countertop, taking deep, slow breaths. *Control yourself. You can never be together.* His brain was right, but the heat below his waist now radiated throughout his whole body and he couldn't think straight. Acting on impulse, he turned and strode back outside and reached for Amanda's hand.

She gave him a look of uncertainty but put her hand inside his.

He pulled her to a standing position.

"Is the pizza almost done?" she asked.

He didn't bother answering. Instead, he put his hand under her chin and pressed his lips against hers with passionate desperation.

She melted into his touch and wrapped her arms around his waist, fully giving in to the tantalizing kiss.

She let out a low sound deep within her throat.

He put his hand on the nape of her neck, then moved it into the depths of her thick hair. The full, deep kiss was everything he'd imagined it would be and more. The spark between them grew until fire and electricity hummed through his veins.

He didn't want to stop but found a small amount of restraint and slowly peeled his lips off of hers.

Her chest rose and fell. "That was ... amazing," she said breathlessly. A throaty sigh escaped her lips. She rested her forehead against his. "But it doesn't change things between us, does it?"

"I don't know anymore. But if I stopped this from happening—whatever this is—I'd regret it."

DOWNSTAIRS, THE FRONT door swooshed shut. Ray turned off the TV and moved his legs to the side of the bed. He had to wait several minutes before standing. Since he'd started chemo, the nerve endings in his feet were damaged. When he finally stood, his limbs felt stiff. He inched toward the window. Hank followed him, nudging his nose against Ray's hand. He patted the greyhound's head, then pulled back the curtain.

In the driveway, Ethan's headlight created a beam across the house, until he backed up and his motorcycle disappeared into the darkness.

The young doctor had stayed much later than Ray had anticipated. A good sign. It seemed like Ethan was doing a good job preventing Amanda from worrying too much.

That was why Ray had stayed upstairs to let Amanda and Ethan have dinner alone. Amanda spent far too much time fussing over him, so he didn't mind the alone time. He'd eaten a sandwich in bed, watched reruns of *Deadliest Catch*, and even snuck a beer out of the kitchen while Amanda and Ethan were outside. Amanda would flip if she knew he'd had alcohol, but he wanted to celebrate the good news about his health.

Since the appointment at the hospital, he'd held on to Ethan's words like a kid clutching a balloon on a windy day. Chemo was working. He might beat cancer and get his life back on track. Work more hours at the Canine Palace and stop relying on his business partner to manage the store. Meet up with buddies at Val's Diner every Saturday instead of taking a morning nap. Rake the yard and trim the bushes, and tell Amanda to take a break for once.

Just thinking about returning to normalcy brought him back to life, refueling his energy. Even at ten o'clock at night.

He walked downstairs to turn off the outside lights. Amanda had left them on. Hank followed at his heels.

His old dog never left him alone anymore. The month before Ray's diagnosis, Hank had stopped lounging on the couch or sunbathing on the deck, completely preoccupied with staying near Ray. Old Hank must have sensed that something was wrong.

Scratching behind Hank's ears, Ray scanned the living room and kitchen. No sign of Amanda. She must've gone to bed already. He turned off the front porch light and walked to the back of the house. The outside light illuminated the deck, where Amanda reclined in the swing, staring out at the river.

He put his hand on the door handle without opening it, so he didn't disturb her. She looked so much like her mother—the blond curly hair, the freckle above her lips, how she wrinkled her nose when she tasted a food she didn't like, and the way she loved taking care of others.

Hank's ears stood on alert. Barking, he lifted a paw and scratched at the sliding glass door.

Amanda glanced in their direction.

Sighing, Ray opened the door, and Hank dashed away, probably chasing a rabbit. Ray stepped out onto the deck and eased down on the swing next to Amanda. "What are you still doing out here, Minnow?" he asked.

"Just thinking." She didn't look him in the eye, her cheeks tinting pink. "Can I ask you a question?"

"Anything."

"Do you believe in 'the one'?"

This had to do with Ethan. She'd never asked a question like this when she'd been dating Tyler. The young doctor was making quite the impression on his daughter.

"Dad, did you hear me?"

He ran a hand over his beard. "I don't know about 'the one,' but I think your mom was the perfect woman for me."

Amanda bent her legs, pulling her knees up to her chest. "Even with Mom's depression?"

"Your mom's depression didn't define her. She was also loving, compassionate, outgoing … And she loved being a mom more than anything else in this world." His took off his glasses and wiped the lenses with his handkerchief. "I'd never understood the whole 'eye sparkling' analogy until the first time she held you and Caleb in her arms."

Amanda smiled, but it fell quickly. "How did you cope when her depression got worse?"

"It didn't happen overnight. It was a slow progression." He wiped the lenses harder. "For many years, your mom hid it from me."

"Why would she do that?" Amanda's brows pinched together, just like when she was a little girl, trying to figure out how to tie her shoes. "Wouldn't Mom want you to know, so you'd understand what she was going through?"

Ray adjusted the glasses over his nose, meeting Amanda's gaze. He put his arm around the back of the swing. "Sometimes, people hide things from loved ones to protect them."

Amanda blinked, then stared at him for a moment, her unwavering gaze intensifying. "Do you hide things from me? Like how you're really handling your diagnosis?"

He tugged on his earlobe.

Hank ambled back onto the deck, his tongue hanging out. He flopped down, resting his head on Ray's foot.

"Every time I bring up cancer, you tell me you're fine. But you can be honest with me. Not knowing is scarier than anything you can tell me."

He shook his head. Amanda was wrong. She didn't know what it was like to be a parent yet. It was better to keep his fears hidden from her. His fear of dying. His fear of suffering. His fear of how his death would affect Amanda and Caleb.

He'd already seen what their mother's death had done to them. After Barbara died, Amanda had started partying in high school. He'd been the one to stop her, to ground her for most of senior year. But if he died—especially after trying chemo—Amanda's heart would shatter. Who would be there to pick up the pieces?

And then there was Caleb. After Barbara's death, his son had stopped caring about school. He'd skipped classes, letting his grades sink. If Ray died, how would Caleb react now? What if he got distracted during a flight and lost control of his aircraft? Or what if Caleb never returned home and continued enlisting in the air force, becoming a lifer? Serving the country was an honorable career, but Ray wanted Caleb to experience life after the air force, too.

These worries plagued Ray, rotting away at his hope, decomposing his mind worse than any chemo treatment could break apart his immune system. He refused to plague his children too. "I appreciate your concern, but there are some things I'd rather keep to myself." He squeezed Amanda's hand three times.

"Okay," she said in a quiet tone.

He cracked his neck from side to side. She'd asked him to open up and he'd completely shut her out. He had to tell her something. "I'm glad the chemo is working. I needed to hear that."

"I did, too." Amanda gave him a weak smile. "I wish you didn't need chemo at all, though."

"You can't control everything in life. Sometimes, you need to let things play out." The moment he said it, he realized he needed the reminder too. Whatever was going on between Amanda and Ethan was out of his control at this point.

But a sinking sensation plummeted to the bottom of his gut. Ethan was only doing what Ray had asked him to do, but Ray had never thought Amanda would go for Ethan, mainly because she'd been so distraught over Tyler. This wasn't supposed to happen. He didn't want his daughter to get hurt.

Chapter 12

AMANDA PLOPPED HER little, round pumpkin in the middle of the face-painting table. Reaching inside a cardboard box, she selected several small brushes and two multicolored sets of paint. She laid half of the materials on Kendall's side of the table and the other half on hers. She couldn't wait for the fall festival to begin.

She looked up from the face-painting station. Committee members were scattered across the farm setting up their stations, hanging signs and banners, and decorating the barn. Ethan stood at the entrance of the corn maze, adjusting a wooden "face in the hole" board that looked like a big stalk of corn. Kids would love peeking their heads out of the hole to take pictures.

Ethan glanced over at her and winked.

Her stomach catapulted through her abdomen.

"When you're done staring at Romeo, we need to finish setting up." Kendall waddled over to the face-painting table, carrying two folding chairs.

Amanda jumped, then tried to recover. She dropped

paintbrushes into jars with fake orange leaves glued to the sides. "I'm not staring."

Rolling her eyes, Kendall unfolded four chairs and set them next to the table, where kids would sit to get their faces painted. "I've never seen you like this before. You're like a teenager with a crush."

Heat flushed beneath Amanda's cheeks. "I don't know what you're talking about."

"You should just kiss him. See if there's any chemistry."

Her cheeks grew warmer.

Kendall's eyes grew wide. She put her hands on her hips, which made her belly appear larger. "You kissed him and didn't tell me?"

Amanda shrugged, pretending it was no big deal. But now that Ethan had kissed her, she had no idea what she was going to do. How were they supposed to go on as friends after a kiss like that—one that left her weak in the knees, igniting desires she'd never known existed?

She licked her lips and refused to look at Kendall. "It's not like anything serious will come out of this. It was a onetime thing."

"Who says it needs to be anything serious?" When Amanda didn't answer right away, Kendall continued. "You need to let go and have some fun."

"I'll think about it," she said dryly. She opened a stack of face-painting images and organized them neatly on the table.

"I can tell I'm really getting through to you." Kendall shook her head, her voice drenched in sarcasm. "Have you seen Grace lately?"

"No, not since I found out about her son."

"I still can't believe she was pregnant that summer. Do you think Liam could be Caleb's kid?"

One of the face-painting images dropped out of Amanda's hand and fluttered to the ground. "I hope not. For Caleb's sake."

"But if Liam isn't Caleb's son, then Grace cheated on your brother. Probably with someone we went to high school with."

"I know." Amanda frowned. "It's horrible either way. If Caleb is the father, he would be devastated to find out he had a son all this time."

Sometimes, people hide things from loved ones to protect them. Maybe Amanda had judged her childhood friend too harshly. Instead of thinking about what Grace went through, Amanda had only been thinking of herself and Caleb. Grace had been a single mom for nine years. That couldn't have been easy.

But was pregnancy the only reason Grace had left or was there more to it? And if Dad's theory *did* apply to Grace, who was she protecting—Liam or her own reputation?

Amanda's first tiny customer kept her from pondering Grace's decisions any longer. She snatched up a paintbrush and went to work.

Two hours later, Amanda could finally relax.

"You have to try the honey lemonade. It's to die for." Amanda handed a cup to Ethan. With the rest of the evening free, there wasn't anything else to do but enjoy the time with Ethan.

He tipped the plastic cup against his lips and took a long drink. "Wow. This is delicious."

"Dill, who owns the grocery store, is also a beekeeper. He makes his own honey."

"We'll have to come back for seconds."

A crowd gathered beneath a tent, cheering and clapping. Amanda and Ethan stopped at the back of the crowd, watching as Kendall's husband, Zach, beat Dill in a pie-eating contest.

Nearby, Kendall whooped and clapped her hands. A smile stretched across her face as she cheered for Zach. One of her hands dropped to rest on her belly, and Kendall's smile faltered. Fine lines of tension appeared in her face. The expression flickered when Zach jogged up to her. Moments later, Kendall squealed with laughter as he kissed her, smearing her cheeks with apple pie.

Amanda couldn't help but chuckle at the couple's antics but she couldn't shake the sense that something was going on with her friend. She made a mental note to ask Kendall about it.

Ethan nudged her in the ribs. "Let's check out some of the other stuff."

They walked from station to station, sipping on their honey lemonades. They bobbed for apples, walked through the corn maze, and stopped to talk to Charlie and Mac, who had brought baby Emma. Amanda leaned over the stroller, running her hand over Emma's plump, rosy cheeks. The infant looked so healthy now, it was amazing to think of all that she'd been through already.

The sun began its descent, and the crowd made its way into the barn. Amanda and Ethan waved good-bye to Charlie and Mac, who needed to take Emma home to sleep.

Inside the barn, Dad walked toward them, waving. His face looked pale. "Hey, you two."

Amanda put her hand on his forearm. "Are you feeling okay?"

Nodding, Dad's voice faltered. "I'm fine."

Ethan's eyebrows creased together. "Take it easy tonight, Ray."

Dad waved his hand dismissively. "Yeah, yeah, I know."

Before Amanda could say anything else, Sandy stopped beside them and turned her attention to Dad. "Since when did you stand around and talk during a hoedown, Ray Meyers?"

Amanda smirked. "If you want to dance with my

dad, why don't you just ask him?"

"You two aren't any better. Young people shouldn't stand on the sidelines." Sandy made a *tsk* noise and pointed a long, curved fingernail at Ethan. "I'm not the only one who needs to ask for a dance." Her smile widened like a Cheshire cat before she wrapped her arm around Dad's. "Come on, you old fool. Let's see if we can get our hearts racing."

As they turned toward the dance floor, Ethan called after them, "Don't forget what I said, Ray."

With Dad and Sandy far enough from earshot, Amanda turned toward Ethan. He looked undeniably handsome in tattered blue jeans, a white T-shirt, and an unbuttoned plaid shirt hanging over it. "Thank you for looking out for my dad. It means a lot to me."

"Of course." Ethan pushed thick, dark hair off of his forehead. "Your dad's a great guy. Everyone in this town loves him. I can't count the number of cards and flowers he gets at the hospital."

She blinked, pride swelling within her. "See, I told you Maple Valley takes care of its own."

"I see that."

The band warmed up onstage before giving a few shout-outs to some of the people who had organized the fall festival, including her. When they finished, they played their own version of George Strait's, "You Look So Good in Love." Several more couples moved out onto the dance floor.

Ethan moved closer, whispering in her ear, "Would you like to dance?"

The moment his lips brushed against her ear, her heart raced at full speed.

She had to work at keeping her voice steady. "Sure, we could take a stab at it."

"It sounds like you want me to stab something, but I'm guessing you mean dancing?"

She giggled. "Yes, that's what I meant."

Grinning, Ethan led her onto the dance floor. He rested his hands on her hips and swayed to the rhythm of the song.

She wrapped her arms around his neck, inhaling the familiar scent of his cologne.

Ethan pulled her even closer, their hips brushing.

Tingles skipped down her spine. Her fingers played with his hair and his thumbs caressed her lower back.

She peeked a glance at his lips, then couldn't look away. She tipped her head up and met his gaze.

He brought his face inches away from hers.

She waited for her senses to come back. She knew better this time. One kiss was bad enough—she'd never forget it.

His lips parted, the longing in his eyes matching her own. He wanted to kiss her again.

Oh heck. One more time wouldn't hurt.

She pressed her lips against his, the kiss soft and tender. He opened his mouth and hers followed as they explored their chemistry without a care in the world.

They were playing with fire, sure to get burned. Ethan couldn't date her. Just like Tyler, Ethan shouldn't be kissing her. But unlike Tyler, she couldn't stop Ethan if she tried.

AMANDA PULLED A black tablecloth off a table inside of Bishop's barn. So far, the committee had torn down all of the outside stations, leaving the barn for last. She folded the tablecloth, then stuffed it inside a large box. Ten more tables to go.

Tearing down was the least fun job of planning any event, but today she welcomed the manual work. It gave her the opportunity to daydream about Ethan. The way he'd held her close on the dance floor and the soft, tender kisses they'd shared throughout the night.

Tyler gave a heavy sigh as he ripped off a tablecloth nearby.

"You okay over there?"

He scowled at her remark, stuffing the tablecloth into a cardboard box. "Did you have fun at the festival?" he asked dryly.

"Yeah." She shrugged and bit back a smile. "I didn't

see you there. Were you in Chicago?"

"I was here. You probably didn't notice me with your face plastered to Ethan's."

Amanda pushed back her shoulders and crossed her arms.

"I thought you said you weren't dating Ethan."

She opened her mouth, then closed it. Several snarky remarks came to mind. They weren't dating and she wasn't going behind Tyler's back. And yet, even if they weren't together, she wouldn't want to see Tyler with someone else either. Not this soon after breaking up. "I'm not."

"Oh, I get it. You're just kissing him."

A few feet away, Kendall stopped sweeping to look in their direction.

Amanda walked closer to Tyler, gritting her teeth. He'd crossed the line. "You're the one who wanted to break up with me, remember?"

He turned around to face her, his voice quiet. "I wanted time apart to *think*."

"About what?"

"I'm not ready to tell you yet."

Another secret. "Give me one good reason I should wait around for you, then," she said through clenched teeth.

Tyler froze for a moment. The only visible sign of movement was the tick in his jaw. After a minute, he closed the distance between them. He cupped his hands on her cheeks, his expression serious. "I still love you. I promise I'll tell you everything soon. And when I do, it'll all make sense."

Her eyes widened. This was the validation she'd been waiting for. But now that she knew how he felt, she was more confused than ever. He still loved her and she loved him, but it didn't feel the same anymore.

Because of Ethan. He was outgoing and charming, encouraging her to do new things like going on the River Boat Cruise or riding a motorcycle. And even though their opinions on healthcare differed, he was the type of oncologist who cared about his patients so much that he'd moved to a new country to learn new procedures. He was also the one who'd been there for her, giving her support when she needed it most. With Caleb being deployed, taking care of Dad felt like her sole responsibility. Ethan's support meant more than he would ever know. It filled a void that she hadn't even realized was there.

If only she could pretend her feelings for Ethan weren't growing stronger. But she couldn't lie to herself. She liked Ethan.

She liked Ethan far too much.

Chapter 13

A WEEK LATER, Ethan ducked his head inside the back seat of his car to throw in his casting rod and bait. Ray had invited him to go fishing tomorrow. He looked forward to going out on the river again, but he couldn't deny he wanted to go for a different reason than fishing. Amanda was coming with them.

The back door to the house opened and his uncle stepped outside and headed across the yard. Orange and red leaves crunched beneath his tennis shoes. He put his hand above his eyes, blocking out the sun and meeting Ethan's gaze. "Do you have a second?"

"Yeah. What's up?" he asked, biting back a smile. The longer he lived here, the more American he sounded.

Uncle Cameron stopped in the driveway. He dropped his hand, exposing the anger in his steel-gray eyes. "Poseidonas has their annual audit going on right now, and one of the auditors found several questionable invoices. They think it could be fraud."

Fraud? Ethan gripped the fishing pole with sweaty palms. "They think someone's stealing money from the company?"

"Yes. They plan on talking to the two bookkeepers first. Raechel's father believes it was Adrian. Your dad doesn't believe your cousin did it. The only other suspect is Raechel, but your dad doesn't believe it's her either. Still, if he questions Raechel, it could get ugly between our families."

Ethan swallowed hard as he contemplated a response, but nothing came to mind. Nothing he could share with his uncle, anyway.

"Are you okay? You look sick."

"Yeah, I, uh … I hope it's a fluke. I don't want any reason for our families to stop doing business together."

"Me either." His uncle glanced down at the fishing pole. "I used to fish when I first moved here. I can't find the time anymore. Are you going with somebody?"

Amanda's image surfaced to the forefront of his mind—dancing with her at the festival, the faint scent of her lilac perfume engulfing his senses as they kissed.

Amanda was amazing. She was family-oriented, caring, and committed. She loved people and she fought for what she wanted. He couldn't stop imagining the way she crinkled her nose when she laughed or how she bit her lip before she kissed him.

Uncle Cameron cleared his throat.

"Haven't we talked about relatives being too nosy?"

Uncle Cameron gave Ethan a knowing look. Shaking his head, he waved good-bye and walked back toward his house.

A minute later, Ethan opened the guesthouse, the silence gnawing at his nerves. Even when it had been just him and Raechel, their home had never been quiet. They had lived downtown, sandwiched between the sea and the city.

He turned on the TV in the living room, then flipped to a soccer game. He plopped on the couch and watched the game for a few minutes, but the game wasn't enough to drown out his concerns.

If anyone discovered who had taken the money, it could threaten the merger. Without it, his parents would be stuck in debt and they'd lose a company that meant everything to them.

Ethan slumped forward, holding his head in his hands. He should have been honest with his parents from the very beginning. But he'd kept quiet, and now his family would pay the consequences.

AMANDA LIFTED THE tip of her fishing pole, watching the bobber go up and down in the river. Little ringlets grew into a big circle, but no other movement surfaced across the water. Frowning, she glanced up at the sunny, cloudless sky.

Normally, she enjoyed warm fall mornings but not on a fishing day. The warm temperature pushed fish deeper into the river and she didn't want to go out too far in case Dad got sick again. He'd argued at first, but Ethan had agreed with her, so Dad had relented.

Out of the corner of her eye, she watched Dad cautiously. Slouching forward in his seat, he rested a fishing pole against his hip and stared at their cabin on the shore, seemingly deep in thought.

Ethan looked at Dad, concern etched across his face. "Ray, are you okay?"

Her chest swelled with gratitude. Ethan was observant enough to tell when Dad wasn't himself.

"Are you okay?" Ethan asked again and patted Dad's knee. "We can head in if you want."

"No. I want to stay for a bit longer." Dad gave them a weak smile. "Unless you young'uns have somewhere else to be."

Ethan shook his head. "I'll stay out here as long as you want."

Ray tipped his hat, but his smile quickly disappeared. It turned into a frown, deepening the wrinkle lines around his mouth.

Her shoulders drooped. She'd hoped fishing would rejuvenate him physically and emotionally, but the last chemo treatment had taken a toll on his energy and attitude. Under the brim of his hat, dark bags hung beneath his eyes. This was exactly why she'd been afraid of him doing chemotherapy.

Over Dad's shoulder, Ethan glanced at Amanda, then turned to face the river. He reeled in his line and cast in a different spot.

She chewed on the inside of her cheek. Ethan had said very little today. Every so often, he would squeeze the back of his neck as if he had a lot of tension in his shoulders. She couldn't help wondering if he regretted kissing her, especially at the festival in front of so many people. A lump formed in her throat.

Something splashed into the river. Her head shot in the direction of the noise as the tip of Dad's pole slipped into the murky water.

His eyes rolled to the back of his head and he mumbled incoherently. He slumped forward, over the boat.

Adrenaline pumped through her veins. She jumped out of her seat. "Dad!"

Ethan lunged, grabbing Dad's waist before he could fall into the water. Dad looked like a rag doll in Ethan's arms. "Ray, can you hear me?"

No answer.

Her heart pounded hard against her chest. She reached for her cell phone and dialed 9-1-1. As she spoke with the dispatcher, she positioned the phone between her ear and shoulder, then moved to the back of the boat and started the engine.

Ethan gently lowered Dad into his lap and put two fingers on Dad's wrist. Ethan looked up at Amanda. "He has a pulse."

Nodding, she directed the boat back to shore. Dad's head flopped forward, his chin bobbing up and down against his chest as the boat sped across the waves.

Two hours later, Dad lay asleep in the ER bed. He had oxygen tubes resting below his nostrils, several wires connected to his chest to evaluate his heart, a blood pressure cuff on his arm, and a pulse oximetry device on his finger to measure the oxygen in his blood.

Amanda perched on the edge of his bed, leaving little space between them. She pulled lightweight blankets up to his chest, tucking him in as if he were a small child. He must be cold with all those fluids pumping through his body. With every fiber of her being, she wished she could protect him from cancer.

But everything she'd done—cleaning the house, diffusing essential oils, and cooking healthy meals—wasn't enough. She rubbed her temples as exhaustion crawled through her brain. What else could she possibly do? There had to be something because she would not allow cancer to take Dad away from her. She knew it was unrealistic to think that way, but the alterative made her feel helpless.

She kissed Dad's forehead, the warmth of his skin comforting to her soul. What had caused him to faint? Most likely it was a side effect from chemo. Ethan had left the room thirty minutes ago to speak with a nurse and get answers, but he wasn't back yet.

She chewed on her thumbnail. Ethan had been so certain that Dad should do invasive treatment. A wave of bitterness dissipated some of her gratitude for Ethan, causing it to disappear as quickly as Dad's fishing pole in the river.

But at least Ethan had gone fishing with them today. He'd been the one to catch Dad, preventing him from falling in the water. If Ethan hadn't been there, Dad could've drowned.

He could've … She stopped herself from thinking the word, but then it came anyway. *Died.*

Moisture built in her eyes and a tear slipped down her cheek. She quickly wiped it away as footsteps approached.

Ethan walked through the door and pulled back the curtain, his expression unreadable.

"What did you find out?" Amanda stood so quickly she felt light-headed.

"His pulse has stabilized and he doesn't have a fever. But his blood sugar is low and he's dehydrated. The fluids in the IV will help significantly."

"Is that why he fainted?"

"Most likely."

She put a hand over her chest. "Thank God."

"He's not completely in the clear yet. We need to run a few more tests on him." Ethan strode across the space and gently touched her arm. "Are you all right?"

She gave a slow nod, trying to push back her emotions, but more tears slipped down her cheeks. "We shouldn't have gone fishing. I should've told him no. I should've …"

"Don't doubt yourself." He pulled her close, cupping her head against his chest. "You were amazing—calling 9-1-1, speeding us back to shore, and docking the boat." He pulled back slightly, his eyes gleaming with admiration. "I'm sure you were scared, but I couldn't tell."

She sniffled. "I don't remember all of it. I think I reacted on autopilot."

"I can see how you'd be a good wife … I mean, *midwife*." Smiling at his mistake, he wiped her tears away with his thumb. "What I meant was, you're calm under pressure."

Amanda laughed, her bottled up adrenaline turning to relief. Dad would be okay for now. She tilted her head, leaning into his gentle touch. "Ethan, don't let my dad die."

Ethan kept his hand on her face, his thumb gently caressing her cheek. He opened his mouth, then closed it, making no attempt to speak again. Fear filled his eyes.

Dread sunk to the pit of her stomach like a heavy anchor. Ever since Ethan had diagnosed Dad, Ethan had seemed confident with the treatment plan. But she knew that look all too well. It was the same look she gave parents when she didn't know if a baby would live. It meant Ethan wasn't so certain Dad would recover.

A bitter taste filled her mouth. She shouldn't be disappointed or surprised by this, but she was.

Somewhere along the way, she'd started to trust that things might work out.

THE NEXT MORNING, Ethan woke to the heightened sound of voices in Ray's room. He tried to sit up on the couch, but Amanda was leaning on him, her eyes still closed. Amanda hadn't wanted to leave the hospital, so he'd offered to stay with her. They'd stayed up late into the night talking and must've fallen asleep.

One of the nurse's voices carried across the room. "He has a fever of 104."

No. Not a fever. Ethan gently shook Amanda until she opened her eyes. She blinked rapidly and rubbed the little crusties out of her eyes. As she sat up, her hair fell loosely around her shoulders.

For a moment, he forgot where they were and gazed at her. She'd never looked so beautiful.

The moment was broken when Amanda looked over at the nurses, a terrified look in her eyes. "What's going on?" she asked in a groggy voice.

"Your dad has an infection," the nurse answered.

Amanda rushed over to her dad's bed. She spoke to him in a soothing voice, so quiet that Ethan couldn't hear what she was saying.

Ray moaned in his sleep.

Ethan's throat went dry. Any kind of infection for a cancer patient could be deadly.

This was exactly why Uncle Cameron had told Ethan not to get personally involved with patients and family members—because sometimes patients died. Of course, he felt terrible for every single life cut short by cancer. But he wasn't Superman. He could only use knowledge and experience to make the best decisions for his patients.

One of the nurses put her hand on Amanda's shoulder. "We need to run blood work and a culture to determine the source of the infection."

Amanda nodded, then turned around to face Ethan. Her icy glare chilled his bones. "This is what I was afraid of. Chemo tore down his immune system. Now, he can't fight off the bacteria like he needs to."

So Amanda blamed Ethan for Ray's fever. Anger simmered beneath the surface and he had to fight to keep his voice smooth and professional. "I've been doing everything I can to save his life."

"Please leave. It's your day off, so you don't need to be here. I can take care of myself."

"Don't do this. I want to be here."

She noticeably swallowed and crossed her arms. "I don't want you here right now," she said quietly.

His anger dissipated as quickly as it came and dread pinched every nerve ending in his body. If Ray's infection grew worse and he lost his life, not only would Ethan lose a friend, but he would also lose Amanda.

Then again, she'd never been his to begin with.

THE NEXT DAY, Ethan leaned forward, setting his elbows on his desk and resting his head in his hands. Uncle Cameron had just walked in to his office to tell him that Ray had pneumonia. The infection had entered Ray's bloodstream, which had caused him to develop sepsis. He had a one in three chance of dying.

Ethan resisted the urge to leave his office and go straight into Ray's room to comfort Amanda. She'd made it clear she didn't want him around. He understood that she was upset; she hadn't wanted her dad to do chemo for this exact reason, but hopefully she would come to her senses soon. Hopefully, she would see that Ethan was not the enemy. He wanted what was best for

Ray, just like she did.

Uncle Cameron rested a hand on Ethan's shoulder. "I know you're upset, but I have something else I need to tell you."

Ethan slowly raised his head and slumped back against his chair. "What is it?"

"I just got off the phone with your mom."

"What did she say?"

Uncle Cameron tugged at his tie, loosening the knot. "The questionable invoices are definitely fraud."

"How much was stolen?" Ethan's gut hardened as he waited for an answer.

His uncle's lips pressed together in a thin line. "Approximately ten thousand dollars."

The blood rushed to his head. *Ten thousand dollars. Enough to buy …*

No, it couldn't be. But the amount was too much of a coincidence.

Uncle Cameron paced back and forth across the small office. "Raechel's father is livid. He wants to buy out Poseidonas."

"What? That's ridiculous. My dad would never agree to that."

"He didn't."

Ethan's shoulders loosened slightly.

"Not yet, anyway. But Raechel's father hired a lawyer to draft a shotgun agreement. So even though your dad declined the initial agreement, he has thirty days to buy out the company." Uncle Cameron ran a hand through his hair, disheveling the black and gray strands. "If he can't, then he'll have to accept the original offer."

Ethan cursed under his breath. No way could his dad afford to buy out the company, not when his parents were buried in debt. After the merger, his parents had bought a bigger house, new cars, and taken several vacations. He didn't agree with how his parents were spending their money, and yet, they never would've guessed that the merger would fall through. They never would've guessed that Ethan and Raechel would get divorced and cause a rift between their families.

Uncle Cameron stopped pacing and cracked his neck from side to side. A vein pulsed visibly in his forehead. "I wish there was something I could do."

Ethan pinched the bridge of his nose. *He* could do something, or at least convince his ex-wife to do something. But if it didn't work, most of his family members would lose their jobs. Enough with the secrecy.

Later that night, he set a pillow against the headboard of his bed, holding a cell phone to his ear and waiting for Raechel to answer.

She answered on the second ring. "I suppose you're calling because of the shotgun agreement."

"Hello to you, too."

"Am I right?"

He gritted his teeth. Raechel wasn't going to make this easy. "Your father can't go through with this."

"What do you care?" Her voice sounded resigned. "You haven't lived here for almost two years. The people you left behind don't matter anymore."

"I was giving everyone space." Clutching the phone, he tried to keep his voice steady. "And I still care about Poseidonas."

"I do, too."

She had a funny way of showing it. But he wouldn't say that. He didn't want her to get defensive. "I know about the fraud. Ten thousand dollars, to be exact."

The line went silent.

"Please tell them the truth."

"Which part? Our infertility? Or you leaving me when I needed you most?"

Guilt flooded through him. She was right. He should have tried harder to work on things instead of leaving to stay with his sister. "If I could go back, I would have been more understanding about what you were going through." He clutched the phone tighter. "Don't you think it's time to let our parents know about everything?"

"No. I … They wouldn't understand. They'll be furious."

"Look, if we don't say anything, the company will be ripped apart. Is that what you want?"

"No, but I can't tell them."

"Raechel, please."

She expelled a long breath into the receiver. "I'll think about it, okay?"

Without waiting for a good-bye, she clicked off the connection.

Ethan tossed his phone on the bed and collapsed back onto his pillow. Frustration coursed through his veins, but he understood her dilemma. Telling the truth might save the company, but it might also ruin their relationships with their parents. In fact, his parents might not ever speak to him again.

Chapter 14

AMANDA STRODE TO the middle of the high school football field, twisting a microphone in her hand. High above her, the scoreboard read 42 to 13. With this win, the Tigers had made it to the playoffs. Dad would be elated. If only he could be here tonight, but he was still hospitalized.

Her chest felt like an anchor was tied to it, her worries heavier than ever before. Could Dad have avoided sepsis if he hadn't done chemo? Or maybe he was sick because he'd caught something from a customer at the Canine Palace. She should've put her foot down and told him that he couldn't work.

She was mad at herself, but she was also angry with Ethan. He'd given her hope. He'd convinced her that Dad would be okay.

And yet, she missed Ethan more than she'd ever expected. It had been three days since she'd told him to leave the hospital room. Three long, agonizing days without hearing his voice. Without seeing his smile.

Without feeling his arms around her.

But she wasn't ready to talk to him yet. What would she say? *I trusted you with my dad's life, and now he could die. It might already be too late.* It didn't seem fair to say that to him, though. She needed more time to sift through her feelings before she could talk to him rationally.

She stopped at the fifty-yard line, expecting to see some of the crowd filing out of the stadium. It didn't usually take long for the game to end and people to leave. But as she looked up at the stands, every spot was full.

Scanning the bleachers, she put a hand over her chest. All of these people were here for Dad. The high school football team filled an entire section, their uniforms standing out in contrast to the T-shirts the committee had designed. Charlie wrapped his arm around Mac's shoulders. Kendall sat in the front row with Zach and many of their friends from high school. Her hands rested on her belly, which had grown to the size of a large basketball. Sandy, Mark, and the committee filled several rows at the back of the stadium. Tyler sat with them, dressed in a blue sweater and dress pants. He gave her a thumbs-up.

Amanda smiled at him. He'd been at the stadium since early this afternoon, preparing for tonight's event. Not only did he still love her, but he obviously cared about Dad, too.

Her gaze flickered to a man and a woman standing at the farthest side of the stands, behind the railing. Amanda squinted to see who it was. The woman wore a baseball hat low over her forehead. Two long braids hung below the hat, resting in front of her slender shoulders.

Amanda's lips parted. Grace had come? Even if Grace wasn't ready to tell Amanda what had happened all those years ago, her presence meant the world. Grace turned toward the man beside her, nodding at something he said.

Amanda gripped the microphone. *Ethan.* A hard knot twisted in her chest, right next to her heart. She looked away from him and clicked on the microphone, expelling a shaky breath. "Thank you for coming tonight. It means so much to my dad and our family. All of the proceeds from tonight will go toward my dad's treatment and hospital stays."

She slid her finger through the envelope flap. "Tonight alone we've raised …" She pulled out the piece of paper and stared at the amount. She choked back a sob. "Twenty thousand."

Everyone in the stands stood and applauded. Some people cheered. Others pulled out their cowbells and rang them.

Her chest swelled with gratitude. Maple Valley had raised enough to pay for some of their bills. And she had

Tyler to thank for organizing the fundraiser.

SHIVERING, RAY ROLLED onto his side and pulled the sheets up to his neck. He squeezed his eyes shut. Darkness loomed over him like a heavy storm cloud. Was this what death felt like? Was it near? Just in case, he'd called Caleb to see if his son could come home to visit. Caleb said he'd leave as soon as he could.

Ray had always known this day would come eventually but not from cancer. He'd always hoped death would happen when he was really old, peacefully in his sleep after he'd retired, after his big fishing trip. But his chances of that were getting slimmer each day the infection lingered.

"Hey, Dad."

He slowly opened his eyes as Amanda walked in, holding out a piece of paper, a triumphant look plastered across her face.

As she drew near, her face crumbled. She sat on his bed and brushed what little hair he had left off his forehead. "Oh, Dad. You're not feeling any better, are you?"

"I'm fit as a fiddle."

She scowled and held a piece of paper in front of him. "I brought you something. Look at this."

Using all the energy he had, he moved up onto his elbows. "What is it?"

"It's the amount we raised at the fundraiser."

He looked at the donation, his eyes widening in disbelief. "Is this *just* from the fundraiser?"

"Yes. And we've raised eight thousand more on the funding page. Can you believe it?"

"Wow. This is unbelievable. Minnow, we're gonna be okay."

"Financially we're much better off, but your health …" She lowered her chin, her frown deepening. "The chemo ruined your immune system."

"Is this your way of saying 'I told you so'?"

"It's just …" She reached for his hand, placing it between her palms. "You have to walk me down the aisle. See me get married and have children. You'll be the grandpa who spoils my kids and feeds them candy and juice." She laughed a little. "What I'm trying to say is … I can't imagine a future without you."

"Then don't."

"I shouldn't have let you work so much. Maybe if you'd stayed home and rested more, you wouldn't be this sick."

Ray coughed and held his hand over his mouth before he spoke. "When your mom died, I constantly questioned whether I'd done enough. But over the years, I've realized that her depression was out of my control.

None of us could've stopped her. Not me. Not you. Not Caleb."

Amanda looked down at her lap. "I don't know what's worse—knowing we couldn't help her or knowing we helped her in every way we could and it wasn't enough."

Ray winced. Barbara's death still made his chest ache and it pained him even more to know how much her depression had affected Caleb and Amanda. "You were enough. Your mom didn't smile a lot at the end, but have you ever noticed when you look back at pictures that she's smiling in the ones with you and Caleb? She loved you so much."

"It wasn't enough to save her life, though."

"But her relationship with you two was the best part of her life. And you and Caleb are the best part of mine, too." Ray squeezed her hand three times to tell her that he loved her.

"YOU'RE DILATED TO a three and you're also one hundred percent effaced." Amanda tugged at a latex glove, removing it from her hand before she helped Kendall move to a sitting position on the couch.

Kendall pulled her maternity dress down over her legs. "Does that mean I'll go into labor soon, like today?"

"Not necessarily. At thirty-nine weeks, you could go into labor two hours from now or two weeks from now." Amanda walked across the room, turning toward the computer to add Kendall's details into her file. Now that Amanda wasn't facing Kendall, she could stop acting happy and allow the residual frown to creep back onto her face.

Fake it till you make it. That was her motto lately. At least Kendall's appointment was the last one of the day. Then Amanda could go back to the hospital to be with Dad.

On the couch, Kendall groaned. "I'm so uncomfortable. I just want to meet my baby."

Amanda typed into the computer and turned around, pushing back her shoulders and lifting her chin. "You will soon. Just remember, your little man will arrive when he's supposed to. In the meantime, ask Zach to give you plenty of massages."

Kendall tucked a strand of hair behind her ear, a worried expression crossing her face, reminding Amanda of the look she'd seen at the fall festival. She'd been so preoccupied with Dad and Ethan that she'd almost forgotten. "What's wrong?"

Kendall caressed her belly. "What if something bad happens during my labor? After feeling him move and picking out his name … I can't lose him."

"We have a team of women who will take good care

of you. It's important to stay positive, especially during labor without any medication. But if anyone can do it, you can."

"I'm so glad you're the one delivering my baby."

"Me too." Amanda walked to the couch and gently pulled Kendall to a standing position. "I'll see you later, okay?"

"Why are you so eager to get me out of here?"

"I'm not. It's just ..."

Kendall stood still, giving Amanda a long, hard look. "You still haven't talked to Ethan, have you?"

She shook her head.

Kendall put her hands on her hips. "Your dad's infection is not Ethan's fault. You just want someone to blame and Ethan is an easy target."

Amanda recoiled. "That's not true."

"Yes, it is," Kendall said quietly. "I think you're blaming him because it's easier to be mad at him than to think about how sick your dad is."

A lump formed in Amanda's throat. Was her friend right?

"It's also easier to be mad at someone you really care about." Kendall gave her a sad smile. "You said you were just having fun together, but you and I both know it's more than that."

Amanda tried to swallow the lump in her throat, but it wouldn't go away. Sometimes, Kendall knew Amanda better than she knew herself.

She should talk to Ethan tonight. If he wasn't working a shift at the hospital, then she'd talk to him after visiting Dad. She needed to be honest with Ethan. She needed to tell him that she'd messed up, not only for blaming him unnecessarily but because she'd done the one thing she promised she wouldn't. She'd fallen for him.

Chapter 15

ETHAN STEPPED OUT of the shower, wrapping a towel around his waist. His shift started in an hour. The moment he arrived at the hospital, he'd check on Ray. Hopefully, Amanda would be there too. Ethan wanted to respect her wishes, but Amanda was stubborn. It could be several more days before she spoke to him. He refused to wait that long.

Three knocks rapped on the guesthouse door.

"Just a sec." Ethan slipped into black dress pants and a white undershirt. He rushed to the front door and opened it.

Uncle Cameron strode inside, throwing his hands up in a gesture of surrender. "Your dad is giving up the company. He hasn't told Raechel's father yet, but that's the plan."

Ethan's mouth fell open. "He still has a few weeks to decide. Why is he doing it now?"

"Your mom was so upset, I could barely understand her. Something about money issues."

Ethan rubbed his temples. So Raechel hadn't convinced her father to change his mind. Scratch that. She must not have tried at all.

If Raechel wouldn't tell the truth, then he would. He didn't have much time. Most flights from Iowa to Greece took about thirteen hours and this was something he had to do in person. "I need to go home to talk to my parents. If I leave today, I could be back to work within the week."

Uncle Cameron scratched the back of his head. "If you go, I think it would be best if you stayed in Greece."

"But—"

"You're a great doctor and you've been a wonderful asset to our oncology unit. But you only have a month left and you've learned all you can about immunotherapy. Plus, your family needs you."

His shoulders slumped as his uncle's suggestion sunk in. "Leave Maple Valley early? What about my patients?"

"I'll take good care of your patients."

"But Ray has sepsis. I don't want Amanda to think I'm leaving them at such a crucial time."

Uncle Cameron sighed. "Like you said, you should hurry. You have to change your dad's mind before he gives up Poseidonas."

Ethan gave a reluctant nod. "I need to talk to Amanda before I leave, though." He hadn't meant to say it out loud, but it was too late. At least his uncle would understand his medical obligation to her.

"You need to focus and talk to your parents. You could always call Amanda after and explain why you left."

Calling her over the phone didn't seem right. Not after everything they'd shared in the last few months. Not when their last conversation had been Amanda telling him to leave the hospital.

He wanted their good-bye to be so much more. He wanted to hold her, kiss her, and tell her that these last few months had been nothing short of amazing.

But his uncle was right. Ethan couldn't let his family down again. Raechel had left him no choice. He had to go back to Greece and face his family.

AMANDA STEPPED OFF the elevator to the oncology floor and stopped short at the locked doors. She pressed the button for the receptionist.

No answer. As she waited, nervous adrenaline pumped through her veins. How would Ethan react when she told him that she'd fallen for him? Would he be upset, or would he tell her that he'd fallen for her too? Even if he had, she knew it wouldn't change things between them. He would still go back to Greece. And yet, a sliver of hope weaved its way into her heart. What if he decided to stay?

She pressed the button again. No one answered and loud voices carried behind the closed doors. Someone screamed.

Blood pounded in her ears. Something was very, very wrong. Panicked, she pressed the button over and over again. *Please be okay, Dad. Please be okay.*

A muffled voice came across the speaker before the receptionist spoke. "Hello?"

"It's Amanda Meyers."

A shrill beep sounded as the door unlocked and Amanda flung it open.

The screaming grew louder, coming from one of the rooms down the hallway. "No, no, no!" an unfamiliar voice cried.

She rushed toward Dad's room, passing patients as they stuck their heads out of their rooms to check out the commotion. She had to get to Dad, to check on him.

Two doors away from his room, Amanda stopped midstride. The room was full of nurses and doctors. In the open doorway, a man kneeled, pounding his fists on the floor.

Amanda took a step back, her skin crawling. *Someone must have died.*

Swallowing hard, her gaze flickered to the name on the wall: Lydia Evans. Amanda didn't know Lydia personally, but she'd seen Lydia doing chemo in the outpatient room. Amanda had watched Lydia's body withering away each time the woman returned for another treatment.

Acid burned in Amanda's throat. She ran to the public bathroom and bent over the toilet, heaving. She gripped both sides of the toilet. Closing her eyes, she took several deep breaths, wishing she could erase the image of Lydia's husband. If Dad didn't survive, that would be her on the floor, screaming.

Behind closed lids, a new image resurfaced. It was the last time she'd seen Mom. Mom had been lying in an open casket, her features as stoic as a porcelain doll, her still hands clasped together across her waist, her blond, curly hair combed neatly to rest above her unmoving chest.

Amanda shouldn't have looked at Mom in the casket. She couldn't erase that image from her mind. Every time she pictured Mom cheering at a football game, dancing with Dad at the fall festival, or sipping an iced tea on the deck while she scrapbooked, the last image of Mom at the funeral home would creep up like a smothering vine.

Amanda spit into the toilet, walked out of the stall, and washed her face and mouth at the sink. She needed to check on Dad. Surely, he'd heard the screams too.

She walked into his room. He was lying in bed and his cheeks were glistening with tears. He looked up and blinked repeatedly as he wiped the tears away with the back of his hand.

"Oh, Dad." He'd definitely heard the screams. But unlike some of the other patients, Dad wasn't strong enough to get out of bed to see what had happened.

She shut the door behind her, drowning out Mr. Evans' screams. She dashed to Dad's bed, crawled under the blankets, and put her arm over his torso.

"Who was it?" he asked so quietly she almost didn't hear him.

"Lydia Evans."

She heard him gulp. For several minutes, they didn't speak. The soft *drip, drip, drip* from the IV amplified the quiet room. In the silence, she wondered where Ethan was. Had he been in the room when Lydia passed away? He cared so much about his patients; he must be heartbroken.

A half hour later, Dad started snoring. Amanda snuggled closer, feeling the rise and fall of his chest. How much longer did she have with him?

The door opened and Grace peeked her head inside. "Can I come in?" she asked.

"Yes," Amanda said quietly.

Eyeing Dad sleeping, Grace shut the door with a gentle click. "When I told Dr. Rosso I was coming in to talk to you, he wanted you to know they are running late on evening rounds."

"Oh. Okay." Amanda slowly sat up, trying not to wake up Dad. Her mind was reeling. After all the time she'd spent at the hospital, Grace had never come to Dad's room. "What did you want to talk to me about?"

Grace shifted her weight from one side to the other before she tiptoed to the far side of the room and perched on the edge of the couch.

Amanda slid out of bed and sat down beside her old friend, leaving some space between them. "What's going on?"

Grace picked at her nails. "I'm sorry that I moved without telling you I was pregnant."

"Why did you keep it from me?"

"I couldn't imagine facing you and Caleb to tell you what really happened. I didn't think you would ever forgive me."

"Did you cheat on my brother?" Amanda crossed her legs, holding her breath as she waited for an answer.

Grace shook her head, sending brown strands across her slender shoulders. "No, but I thought I had at first."

"I don't understand."

"Remember the night of the senior party? Caleb and I got into that big fight. We were both drunk and in the middle of our fight, your dad found out about the party and took you and Caleb home." Tears watered in her eyes. "I stayed at the party and started playing drinking games. Later in the night …"

Amanda placed a hesitant hand on Grace's shoulder and was surprised when her old friend leaned into the contact. Questions bubbled up but she held them back, giving Grace the chance to continue.

Grace stared down at her hands. "I was raped."

Amanda put a hand over her mouth. Guilt flooded through her. *All those years I was angry and hurting and she was dealing with this.* "I am so sorry, Grace."

"At first, I thought it was my fault. I'm the one who stayed at the party and got drunk. I was a little too flirty because I was mad at Caleb. But I never intended to cheat on him. I loved him." Grace looked up, meeting Amanda's gaze. "It was easier for me to blame myself because at least I had control of the situation. In my mind, anyway. After we moved away, my mom made me see a counselor, and eventually I realized that it wasn't my fault."

Amanda nodded in agreement.

"I wanted to get rid of the baby. I never wanted to think about that night ever again. But my mom raised me as a single parent and she was a great mom. I knew with her help, we could raise the baby together."

"I'm glad you told me."

A tentative smile spread across Grace's face. "I know it was awful of me to run away—"

"Hey, you had a tough decision to make." Amanda understood her reasons. In a small town like Maple

Valley, the whispers would have always followed Grace and Liam. "I'm sure you're a great mom. I'd like a chance for us to reconnect. And to get to know Liam, if that's okay."

Surprise followed by cautious happiness filled Grace's expression. "Really?"

"Really." Amanda leaned over and wrapped her arms around Grace. She couldn't help wondering who the father was. She wanted to ask, but it wasn't the right time.

Grace pulled back from their embrace. "I know this is a little out of the blue, given what we were just talking about, but …" A hint of sadness gleamed in her eyes. "How are you doing now that Ethan's back in Greece?"

Huh? Amanda must not have heard Grace correctly. "What do you mean?"

Grace stiffened. She studied Amanda for a moment before she spoke slowly. "Ethan moved back early. I guess he had to handle something with his ex-wife."

Amanda's stomach coiled. *His ex-wife?*

"I thought he would've told you." Grace stopped speaking, her porcelain skin turning crimson.

Amanda slumped back against the couch in shock. She had pushed Ethan away, but he had to know she didn't mean for him to leave forever. Instead of working it out, he ran back to his ex. She was such a fool to fall for a completely unavailable guy. A guy who'd left without even saying good-bye.

ETHAN APPROACHED HIS parents' house—a large, white home with a flat roof and stone pillars. Beyond the covered courtyard, a long, narrow hill sloped down to the sea below. Seeing his childhood home ignited a homesickness he hadn't felt before. And yet, he needed to handle this situation as quickly as possible so he could call Amanda.

He hadn't had time to call her yet. Just the thought of her made his heart pick up speed. But after speaking with his uncle, he'd quickly packed, sped to the airport, traveled overnight, and rushed here to talk to his family.

He stopped at the end of the long driveway, wiping his sweaty palms against his shorts. This was it. The moment of truth. Would his parents disown him or did he have a chance at reconciliation?

Before he'd left the US and boarded the plane, he'd called Raechel three times. His calls had gone straight to voicemail. So he'd texted her instead. *I'll be home tonight. We need to talk.*

He slowly started up the driveway. Solar lights illuminated a path to a new pool and hot tub. In the fading sunlight, bright lights poured out of the tall, rectangular windows, casting a glow on a shiny black Fiat Spider parked outside the garage. He scowled. His parents had bought a new vehicle *again*?

One of the sliding glass doors was open, revealing loud, excited voices talking over one another. He opened the door farther and stepped into the kitchen, where his parents, sisters, and their families sat at the table, eating dinner. "*Yasso*."

The house went silent.

Dad dropped his fork. It clattered against his plate, sounding far too loud in the suddenly quiet room.

Mom stood and reached for him, then quickly dropped her hand. A pained expression flashed in the deep irises of her dark brown eyes.

His three brothers-in-law looked at him in surprise and nodded in welcome and his nieces and nephews jumped up from the table, flinging their arms around his legs. "Uncle Ethan!"

He bent down and ruffled their hair. "It's good to see you. You're all getting so big." A pang of guilt struck through his chest. His nieces and nephews looked so much older than they had when he'd left. He'd missed a lot in the last couple of years.

Sophia stood and walked toward him, smiling. She cupped her hands over his cheeks. "This is a pleasant surprise. Why are you back early?"

"I'd like the answer to that question as well." Dad sat with his back rigid and arms folded across his broad chest.

Ethan licked his lips. He moved closer to the table, his heart pounding in his chest. He squared his shoulders and gripped the back of a chair. "I can't let you give up Poseidonas."

"You suddenly care about the family company?" Dad asked.

"I always have."

Seeming to lose interest in the conversation, his nieces and nephews ran into the living room, where dozens of toys were scattered across the floor.

Dad folded a napkin over his half-eaten dinner and pushed his plate away. "Why do you care if we give up the company or not?"

"Because you love it. You shouldn't let Raechel's family force you into it."

Mom and Dad exchanged a guilty look. Mom adjusted a diamond bracelet on her wrist. A bracelet that looked far too expensive.

"You're one to talk," Sophia said quietly. "You let Raechel control your entire relationship."

His nostril's flared. "That's not true."

Mom wrapped her hands around the mug in front of her. "When Raechel asked for a divorce, you just accepted it." She drummed her fingers against the mug. "You didn't fight for her at all."

"I had a good reason."

Dad shook his head. "There is no good reason for getting divorced. You could've worked through it and now you've left the merger in shambles."

Ethan gripped the back of the chair so tightly his knuckles turned white. "That's why I came back early. I'll speak to Raechel and ask her to talk to her father. She might be able to convince him to keep the merger."

Footsteps sounded at the door. "Will you now?"

Ethan turned to see Raechel standing in the doorway, her long, ebony hair draped across a thin, white dress that fit a little too snugly across her torso. She'd gained weight in the last few years. "What are you doing here?" he asked.

Raechel strode into the house, her sandals flip-flopping against the tile floor. She kissed him on the cheek, her gesture oddly familiar despite the years they'd spent apart. "I'd ask you the same thing, but I think I know why you're here."

She sat down at the table and crossed her legs. "We have something we need to tell you."

Ethan moved into the open chair next to her, his nerves on high alert. Was Raechel finally ready to tell the truth? He leaned forward, resting his elbows on the table. "Do you want me to start?"

Raechel nodded.

"When we got married, we wanted to start a family right away. But we had a hard time conceiving."

Mom put a hand over her breastbone. "We had no idea."

"We didn't want anyone to know." Ethan shifted in his chair. "It would've put more pressure on us if you knew about our infertility issues."

"*My* infertility issues." Raechel clasped her manicured hands together and set them on the table. "We both had tests done and discovered that I have endometriosis."

"I'm sorry to hear that, dear," Mom said.

His sisters and brothers-in-law nodded as well.

Ethan frowned. His family felt sorry for them. But they didn't know everything yet. "It's not impossible to get pregnant with endometriosis, so we kept trying. But after two years, we decided to try fertility treatments."

Raechel glanced down at her clasped hands. "It was really expensive. We had just graduated from college. We ..." She noticeably swallowed. "I was desperate. So I started taking money from Poseidonas to pay for the treatments."

His sisters gasped.

Mom's mouth hung open.

Dad stared at Raechel as if he couldn't decide if she was telling the truth. When he spoke, his voice was strained. "You're the one who's been taking money?"

Raechel nodded slowly, then hung her head.

Dad stood up so fast, his chair fell over backward. He put his hands on his hips. A moment later, he let his arms fall to his sides, then slammed a fist against the table. His angry gaze flickered to Ethan. "You knew about this and didn't tell us?"

Ethan felt like a teenage boy again, getting in trouble for sneaking out of the house past curfew. "Yes," he answered slowly.

Dad paced back and forth across the room and mumbled under his breath. When he finally spoke clearly, he stopped and put his hands behind his head. "I can't believe it. How could you?"

"Don't blame Ethan. He only knew about the first time. He made me promise never to do it again." She met Ethan's gaze with a look that hinted at regret. But as quickly as he saw it slip, her impassive mask returned. "He had no idea that I hadn't kept my promise until the recent audit."

Beneath dark, bushy eyebrows, Dad's eyes narrowed to slits. "You must've thought you were so clever—creating a fake vendor and fake invoices." He spat the words at Raechel. "Then you waited until the invoices were paid and took the checks, cashing them yourself. Is that right?"

Her bottom lip quivered. "Yes," she said in a quiet tone.

"Get out of my house."

Raechel noticeably swallowed. "I—"

Mom cut her off, her tone gentle but firm. "We need

some time to process all of this."

Raechel nodded. She looked at Ethan, then turned and walked out of the kitchen. The soft click of the front door echoed through the house.

His family stared at him, a mixture of shock and disgust plastered across their features.

"I, uh … I'll be back." He left the room and followed Raechel outside.

She hadn't made it far down the driveway. As soon at the door shut behind him, she turned around, her long, dark hair falling across her face. She didn't bother to push the strands away. "I should've kept my promise. I meant it at the time, but after I started dating again, I knew I'd want to get married and try to get pregnant. I started taking small amounts at a time, so no one would notice."

That was as close to an apology as he would get. "Have you talked to your parents?"

"Not yet. But even when my father finds out about the money, I'm not sure he'll change his mind about the shotgun agreement."

"Why not?"

"After we got divorced, he's never felt like things were right between our families. He's a stubborn man, Ethan."

"We have to fix this."

Her shoulders drooped and she wrapped her arms

around her body, holding on to her elbows. "I can't promise anything."

Her words stung. It might be too late to fix things for Poseidonas.

If he couldn't make a difference, then he'd come here for nothing and leaving Maple Valley had been a mistake. More importantly, leaving Amanda had been a mistake.

Chapter 16

AMANDA STARED OUT the window as sunlight poured into Dad's hospital room. She'd slept at the hospital overnight again, not wanting to be alone. Especially not after talking to Grace. It still didn't seem possible that Ethan was gone, that he'd moved without saying good-bye to her. She'd spent the night tossing and turning on the hard couch, crying quietly so she wouldn't wake up Dad.

Ethan was not the man she thought he was. Just like when Tyler had asked for a break. But at least Tyler had the guts to tell her in person.

A tidal wave of anger took over, and she wanted to dislocate Ethan's ribs on purpose. Okay, not really dislocate his ribs. But she wanted to give him a piece of her mind.

If only he didn't have a piece of her heart. Moisture built in her eyes and tears slid down her cheeks. She grabbed a Kleenex and dabbed at her sore, swollen eyes.

Waking up, Dad turned over on his side and reached

for his glasses on the nightstand. Sliding them over his ears, he looked at her with concern. "What's wrong, Minnow?"

She crumpled the Kleenex in her hand. "Grace told me that Ethan moved back to Greece. He's gone." Her voice shook. "He didn't even say good-bye."

Dad pressed a button on the side rail. The bed made a groaning noise as it moved him to a slanted, sitting position. "I'm sure Ethan had a good reason for leaving."

Amanda wrinkled her nose. "Why are you sticking up for him? Ethan left when you needed him the most. When I needed him the most."

Dad pulled the blankets higher to his chest and tucked them beneath his armpits. He ran his hand over the blankets, straightening out the wrinkles. "I feel like I'm partly to blame."

"What are you talking about?"

He pushed his glasses higher on his nose. "When I first went fishing with Ethan, I asked him to spend time with you. You were so upset after the breakup with Tyler. I thought Ethan would be a good distraction."

Her eyes widened. This took meddling to a whole new level. "How could you?"

"I was worried about you."

She shook her head in disbelief. "So every time I hung out with Ethan, he was just doing it to appease *you*?"

Dad's ears grew red. "Possibly at first, but I know Ethan fell for you. I saw the sparks in his eyes."

"You're wrong." Her heart thudded dully against her chest. Ethan had made a deal with Dad, then hung out with her like she was some meaningless fling. No wonder he'd left without saying good-bye. Just like all the other women he'd dated, she'd meant nothing to him.

AMANDA UNROLLED HER yoga mat in the middle of the living room floor in front of the fireplace. She moved into cobra pose and inhaled the lavender oil diffusing through the room. Since she'd left the hospital this morning, she'd kept busy. She had to be doing something, anything, to keep her mind off of Ethan.

She shifted positions, moving into downward dog. Beside the yoga mat, her phone vibrated. She peeked at the screen to see the caller.

Speak of the devil.

She dropped to the floor and grabbed her phone, debating if she should answer. She didn't want to hear his excuses, and yet, she yearned to hear his voice. She slid her thumb across the screen, accepting the call. "How's Greece?" she asked dryly.

"Amanda." His voice was thick with emotion. "I can explain."

"Don't bother. Grace told me." She clutched the phone tightly to her ear. "In fact, I had an interesting conversation with my dad, too. He told me all about your deal."

The line went silent before Ethan spoke again. "It wasn't like that."

"What was it like, then?"

"I *wanted* to spend time with you. I enjoyed every second."

She chewed on the inside of her cheek. Even now, he was trying to be his charming self. She wasn't falling for it anymore. "And yet, you left without saying a word to me."

"I wanted to see you, but I didn't have time. I had to catch the earliest flight." He blew out a breath into the receiver. "My ex-wife's father was trying to convince my dad to give up their fishing company. I couldn't let that happen, so I came back. I'm the only one in my family who could fix this."

"Why?"

"Well ..." Ethan told her about the secret he'd kept, how he and Raechel had told his family about it, and how badly his parents needed to keep the merger agreement to pay off their debt.

As she listened, she crossed her legs on the mat and leaned forward, plucking at the carpet like tugging weeds out of a garden. "So you *were* hiding something. You moved to Iowa because you didn't want to tell your family that your ex-wife had stolen money." Amanda shook her head. "You're a coward."

The line went silent again before Ethan spoke. "Okay. I deserved that."

"Is that the only reason you called? To tell me why you left, so we can end things and move on?" She hated the bitterness in her tone, but she couldn't help it. Talking to Ethan and hearing his voice was breaking down her wall of shock, and letting reality wash over her, drowning her in the truth. She would never see him again.

"It's not the only reason I called. I also wanted to tell you how sorry I am for leaving so suddenly. It's not how I wanted things to end between us."

"Does it matter?" The moment she asked, she knew she didn't mean it. She was being defensive because his words hurt her, exposing what a fool she'd been. He'd always intended to end it.

"Of course it matters."

She tried not to notice the pain inflected in his tone, so she wouldn't lose her nerve. "You were moving soon anyway. It was fun while it lasted, right?"

"Amanda, I miss you."

Her lips parted. She couldn't deny the raw honesty in his voice. Maybe she was more than a fling. Maybe his feelings were mutual.

But he was in Greece and she was in Iowa. He had an oncology clinic to return to. He had a family who wanted him to marry a Greek woman, if he ever changed his mind and decided to get married again.

They could never be. She'd known that from the beginning. Then he'd complicated things by kissing her. And she'd kissed him back. As mad as she was at Ethan for the way he'd left, she was mostly mad at herself. For falling in love with him.

She choked back a sob. "I have to go, Ethan. Good-bye."

She collapsed against the yoga mat and cupped her hands over her face as tears streamed down her cheeks. Ethan was gone for good. Just like she'd lost Mom. Just like she'd lost Grace.

In her deepest, darkest moments, their absences made her feel like she wasn't enough. Like she wasn't worthy of their love.

She tried to remind herself that it wasn't true. Mom had died because of her depression, Grace had moved because of her pregnancy, and Ethan had never planned on staying. Their choices had nothing to do with her.

But it still hurt. She curled up in a ball as sobs shook her body. In all the times she'd cried over Tyler, she'd never cried this hard. It must be because Ethan's move was the last straw. They'd only known each other for a few months. It couldn't be possible that she loved Ethan more than Tyler.

And yet, her heart had never felt so hollow.

ETHAN STUCK HIS bare feet in the sea, wiggling his toes as the clear blue water rushed over his feet. He watched the sun rise above the horizon and inhaled the salty air. How many days had he woken up to this beautiful view? Too bad he couldn't enjoy it. Not when his conversation with Amanda was churning his stomach like he'd consumed an entire plate of greasy bacon from Val's Diner.

He walked farther into the sea, letting the water rise to his ankles. He should've talked to her in person instead of waiting to call her. He should've told her how he really felt about her. But every time he'd opened his mouth to say it, he'd stopped. Because he didn't know if he'd ever come back to Iowa, and it wouldn't be fair to her.

"I knew I'd find you here."

Ethan turned around. Mom stood on the shore, a yellow dress flowing across her ankles. "Lucky guess," he said.

"Or maybe I know you better than you think. When you're worried about something, you tend to go to the beach. You always said it calmed you down. Is it working?"

"No."

Mom picked up the bottom of her dress and waded out to him. Dark bags accentuated her bloodshot eyes.

His decision to protect Raechel had caused her so much pain. "I should've told you and Dad sooner."

"That's true. But we shouldn't have shut you out, either. I've missed you so much."

"Does that mean you're not mad about the money?"

"Oh no, I'm upset. But I understand why you did it."

Relief flooded through him. This was exactly what he'd been waiting for all along, for his parents to understand.

"I'm glad you're home."

Home. Greece was home. But he missed strolling through downtown Maple Valley and stopping to talk with people who never seemed in a hurry, who genuinely enjoyed knowing how you were doing; attending events like the fall festival and pumpkin patch; going over to his uncle's chaotic house to play hide-and-seek with his cousins.

In the silence, Mom put her hand on his arm. "You are back for good, right?"

"I'm not sure."

She dropped her hand. A moment later, she blinked away tears. "Does this have something to do with the person you were on the phone with last night?"

"Yeah."

She stared at him with misty eyes. "Is it serious?"

"That's the problem. We weren't technically dating before I left."

"But you have feelings for her." Mom sent him a knowing look. "Does she know?"

"Kind of." Ethan dug his feet beneath the soft, wet particles of sand. "She knows I'm attracted to her."

Mom snorted. "So you've never actually told her?"

"No."

"Some things never change."

He stiffened. "What's that supposed to mean?"

"You rely on your charm too much. You act like it's enough, but a woman wants to hear how you feel. Otherwise, she's second-guessing your feelings." The wind blew dark bangs across Mom's forehead. "What is her name?"

Ethan ran his hands through the water. He'd just made amends with Mom and the truth would only reopen new wounds. But he was done keeping secrets from his parents. "Her name is Amanda."

Mom tilted her head. "That's not a Greek name. What were her parents thinking?"

"She's not Greek," he answered slowly.

"Not Greek?" Mom stepped back. Confusion, hurt, then anger flashed across her face. "I don't even know who you are anymore."

As she walked away, Ethan winced. He had to agree with her. Because ever since he'd left Iowa, all he'd thought about was Amanda. He'd never expected to fall for her. She'd crashed into his motorcycle. She'd questioned his cancer treatment suggestions. She'd called him out for dating a lot of women.

But she'd also challenged him in ways that most people were afraid to. She'd encouraged him to open up about his past marriage and hadn't judged him for it. And even though she'd never had a miscarriage, she had a deeper understanding than most people, given her career as a midwife. And somehow, over the last few months, Amanda had made him realize that he shouldn't let go of his dreams to get married and start a family.

And yet, the logical choice would be to stay in Greece. He could pick up where he left off at the cancer clinic and continue building his career. Most importantly, he could reestablish a relationship with his family. Spend more time with his sisters and their families. It made sense.

But could he live with that choice?

Chapter 17

AMANDA WALKED UP the front steps of the cabin in a foggy haze. Her feet ached and her calves burned. Kendall's labor had lasted twenty-six hours. Despite her friend's initial fears about labor, Kendall had delivered an eight-pound, healthy baby boy.

As Amanda neared the steps, her lips parted. A tall vase sat on the stoop with a bouquet of roses inside of it. She leaned over and picked up a small card, sandwiched between the flowers. *I care about you more than you'll ever know.* The sender left no signature and the handwriting didn't look familiar, unless the florist wrote it.

Her heart fluttered. Could these be from Ethan?

She carefully lifted the vase and opened the front door. Inside, she gasped. Roses were scattered across the living room and kitchen floor. She hung her purse on an entryway hook and followed the path of roses out to the back deck.

Opening the sliding doors, she almost dropped the vase. Tyler stood on the deck wearing a navy blue pinstripe suit. His dark blond hair was gelled and his face clean-shaven.

Holy cow. Amanda waved a hand in front of her face. Was he about to do what she thought he would do?

He stepped toward her, took the vase, and put it down on the table. "The weekend we were supposed to go to Florida, my dad didn't need me to go to Chicago."

Her gut hardened. Not exactly what she thought he would say. "Why did you lie to me?"

"My dad is retiring in the spring and he asked me to take over his practice."

Whoa. That possibility hadn't even occurred to her. It would be a great opportunity for Tyler.

He reached for her hands, entwining their fingers. "The reason I didn't tell you is because I know how much you love Maple Valley. I could never ask you to move."

So he hadn't wanted to burden her with that kind of choice. But she would've preferred to know so they could've made the decision together. "What are you going to do?"

Tyler smiled. "I'm not going to take over the practice. I can't imagine my life without you." He tucked a strand of hair behind her ear. "I've had a lot of time to think over the last few months. I know it's taken me a long time to figure it all out, but I promise I'll make it up to you."

Moisture built in her eyes as he got down on one knee. She'd dreamed about this day since the moment she'd fallen in love with him. And now, it was happening.

Tyler lifted a black velvet box out of his jacket pocket. His smile widened. "Amanda Meyers …" He opened the box, exposing a shiny white-gold ring with a large, sparkling diamond. "Will you marry me?"

"Oh Tyler." Tears trickled down her cheeks, the flood of emotions overwhelming her. He *loved* her. He chose to stay in Maple Valley even though he wanted to move back to Chicago.

A ghost of a smile spread across her face, but inside her heart wavered. That was the problem. Could she let him? Would he be happy here for the rest of his life or would he eventually resent her?

Questions plagued her heart as Tyler stared up at her, waiting for an answer. Then it hit her. All of her concerns were focused on Tyler. She couldn't control Tyler's feelings or attitude about living in Maple Valley over Chicago.

But she could control her own feelings. Which only left one question. Would she be happy if she married Tyler?

ETHAN LEFT THE airport, heading straight to the Meyers' cabin. He had to tell Amanda how he felt. Otherwise, he'd regret it for the rest of his life.

He sped down the gravel driveway, halting behind a silver Mercedes. Dust floated around him as he stepped out and peered at the other car. Two stickers stuck to the back window: one was a picture of a spine with *I've got your back. Choose Cory's Chiropractic* and the other read *What happened to "Do No Harm?" Hypocrites. Choose Natural Healthcare.*

Ethan scoffed. What a stupid quote. This had to be Tyler's vehicle. What was Amanda's ex doing here?

He strode past the Mercedes and knocked on the front door. No one answered. He walked around the side of the house, halting in place. Tyler and Amanda stood on the deck, hugging. He thought he heard Amanda crying, but he wasn't sure.

He gritted his teeth as Tyler put his hands on Amanda's cheeks and stared longingly into her eyes. Ethan's stomach felt like he'd just been sucker punched. Amanda and Tyler were back together?

Ethan cursed and marched back to his rental car. Resisting the urge to bang his head against the steering wheel, he started the car and reversed out of the driveway. He never should have left. Raechel's father hadn't changed his mind yet. His parents were upset with him for an entirely new reason. And Ethan's absence had given Tyler the perfect opportunity to swoop in and get Amanda back.

A deer dodged across the gravel driveway right in front of the car. Ethan swerved to miss it. He should've seen it running across the clearing before it got to the driveway, but he'd been too distracted to notice it. He almost smiled at the irony. Just like Amanda had been distracted when she'd crashed into him.

He sped back to Uncle Cameron's house, finding his uncle in the backyard, raking leaves.

As Ethan approached, Uncle Cameron turned around, his eyes widening. "Why didn't you tell me you were coming back? I would've picked you up from the airport."

"I went to the Meyers' first." Ethan frowned. "But Amanda is, uh … She seems preoccupied with someone else at the moment."

Bending over, Uncle Cameron picked up a pile of leaves and dropped them into a yard waste bag. "You mean with Tyler?"

"Yeah. How did you know?"

"Tyler was at Val's Diner this morning showing off the engagement ring he'd bought for Amanda. He was planning on proposing sometime today."

The blood rushed out of his face. Tyler and Amanda weren't just dating again. They were engaged.

Ethan shook his head. She'd told him that she would

take Tyler back. He never should've taken the risk of coming back to Iowa without talking to her first. Without knowing how she felt about him. Even though they'd fought the last two times they'd spoken, he'd foolishly thought that they would make amends, just like they always did.

But he'd been a fool to think she would wait around for him, especially when she thought he was never coming back. So much for surprising her. So much for telling her how much she meant to him.

AMANDA OPENED THE curtains in Dad's hospital room, letting in the sunlight. Her engagement ring reflected off the wall. She'd told Tyler she needed time to consider his proposal, and he'd told her to wear the ring while she thought about it.

Warm sunlight spread across her back as she turned around and retrieved a homemade smoothie from the fridge. She handed it to Dad, then called downstairs to order him breakfast. How odd that this morning routine had become normal. That this hospital had stopped feeling like the evil monster that had swallowed Mom whole and become a place of hope.

Ethan had made it feel safe. And now that Dad had sepsis, it was the only place that could save his life.

Ethan's uncle, Dr. Rosso, knocked on the door before entering the room. "Good morning. I have news for you."

Amanda hung up the phone, her hands suddenly trembling. *News? About Dad's infection?*

The doctor strode across the room and stopped at the edge of the bed. He handed Dad a piece of paper.

Amanda rushed over to the opposite side of the bed and peered down at the paper. But her nerves prevented her from reading it clearly. She looked up. "What does it all mean?"

Dr. Rosso smiled. "The infection is gone."

Amanda tilted her head back. She closed her eyes and covered her mouth as relief washed over her body, replaced with joy. "I can't believe it." Opening her eyes, she bent down and hugged Dad. "You're okay."

Behind his glasses, Dad's eyes glistened. It looked like he wanted to say something, but he grinned instead.

With her arms wrapped around Dad, she felt a mixture of emotions. As happy as she was, this news made her miss Ethan even more. If only Ethan were here to see Dad's progress.

If only Ethan were here for her. So she could tell him how he'd changed her. How she'd been too closed-minded about healthcare. Sometimes, there were benefits to traditional medicine. How she'd been stuck in her daily routine and small-town life until he'd pushed her to try new things. Like riding a motorcycle. Like going on the River Boat Cruise.

Dr. Rosso took the paper back and slid it into a folder. "We'll wait and give your body a break and also let your blood counts come back up before we administer your next round of chemo."

Dad nodded. "Great."

"With that said, you get to go home today." Dr. Rosso squeezed Dad's shoulder. "Please give us a call right away if you have another fever, abnormal swelling, pain, or if you develop a cough."

"Of course."

"Do you have any questions for me?"

Still grinning, Dad shook his head.

Amanda chewed on her thumbnail. This had nothing to do with Dad's health, but she had to know. "Have you talked to Ethan lately?"

Dr. Rosso scrubbed a hand over the stubble on his face. His lips drew into a line thin. "Yeah, I have. I just spoke with him this morning in my office."

She bit down harder on her nail, causing the skin beneath it to bleed. "I thought he was in Greece."

"He's back." Dr. Rosso sighed. "Look, Amanda. You're sweet. But whatever was going on between you and Ethan had to stop eventually. You'd just put more strife between him and his family."

Her lungs constricted, making it difficult to breathe.

He'd come back to Maple Valley? Nauseous waves rolled through her stomach. "I, uh, I need some air."

She hurried out of the room and down the hallway, then took the steps two at a time. She had to get out of here. She pushed open the lobby door and sagged against the outside wall.

The family sitting outside at one of the tables looked over and stared at her.

Amanda didn't care.

She bent forward and buried her head in her hands. Ethan was back and he hadn't tried to see her. He must not have missed her *that* much. She was sick of him toying with her emotions, playing with her heart. In fact, she was through with him.

Straightening, she twisted the engagement ring on her finger. She needed to stop wishing that she and Ethan had a chance and focus on her future. A future that didn't include Ethan.

Chapter 18

ETHAN PARKED HIS motorcycle outside of his uncle's guesthouse. He took off his helmet, the cold air stinging his face. Despite the cold, he opened the storage container attached to his bike and pulled out a spiral notebook. He ran his fingers along the metal spiral.

Lydia wanted you to have this. Mr. Evans had given Ethan the notebook this afternoon at her wake. On the inside of the cover, Lydia had left a note: *Ethan, when you find your forever someone, use this to write her love notes on your anniversary.*

He swallowed hard, remembering one of his last conversations with Lydia. She'd told him not to live as if his life was sand running through an hourglass. Oddly enough, since discovering that Amanda was engaged, he hadn't felt like time was running out at all. He felt like time had stopped. It didn't seem to matter anymore.

After his visa was done, he would fly back to Greece and teach his colleagues at the clinic everything he'd learned. There was no reason to stay anymore.

He walked to the guesthouse and reached for his keys when he noticed the door was slightly ajar. He must've forgotten to lock it, or maybe his cousins were trying to play a prank on him.

Ethan stepped inside cautiously, scanning the room. He dropped his keys on the welcome mat as he stared at his two visitors, who were sitting on the couch. "What are you doing here? How did you get in?"

Mom smirked. "Your uncle let us in. And what does it look like we're doing? We came to see you."

Dad held his hands up in innocence as if being here was Mom's idea.

Shutting the door, Ethan walked farther inside the guesthouse. "You know I'm flying back soon, right?"

"No, you're not," Mom said. "Why don't you sit down?"

Ethan unzipped his leather jacket and squeezed in next to her on the couch. What was going on? Why did they come all the way from Greece?

Dad leaned forward, putting his elbows on his knees. "Raechel's father wants to keep the merger."

Ethan almost jumped up from the couch. "What changed his mind?"

"Raechel." Dad spoke excitedly. "She's pregnant."

"What?" Ethan's eyes grew wide. That explained her weight gain. "That's great."

"Her father is so excited to be a grandpa that he

realized he needed to stop being mad at you and our family for the divorce." Dad suddenly grew somber. "Of course, she's not working for the company anymore."

Ethan nodded. Probably a good call.

Mom shifted on the couch, putting her hand on his knee. "Now we have another issue to discuss."

Here it comes. The argument about why he should date a Greek woman. He squared his shoulders, bracing for impact.

"These last few years, barely speaking to you … they've been terrible. I hated every minute, and I won't do it again."

"I have too."

"I don't agree with you dating or even marrying a non-Greek woman, but I refuse to lose you again."

His lips parted. They didn't agree with his decision, but at least they weren't mad. Not that it mattered now. Amanda was taken.

Mom cupped her hands on his face, smashing his cheeks. "This Amanda lady, she better be a woman worth fighting for this time."

He pulled back from her grip as Mom's words sunk in and stirred up his heart. Amanda was definitely worth fighting for. And what was he doing? Just giving up. Why would he let Tyler take her away from him?

"Well, is she?"

"Yeah, she is." Adrenaline pumped through his veins.

He stood quickly and pushed back his shoulders. "I have to go."

Dad tilted his head to the side. "Where are you going? We just got here."

Ethan zipped up his leather jacket, laughing as Mom playfully slapped Dad's thigh. "To fight for her, you dummy."

IN THE DISTANCE, the sun began its descent, coloring the sky with orange and pink hues. Amanda shivered and reeled in her empty line. The fish had taken her worm. She reached for the little Styrofoam container sitting on the seat between her and Dad on the boat. Now that he was feeling better, she promised she'd go fishing with him one last time before winter moved in.

Dad's eyebrows furrowed together as he fixed his gaze on something behind her. "Is that Caleb? Maybe he finished his errands early and decided to join us."

She hoped Dad was right. It was so nice to have her brother back in town, even though she hadn't figured out how to break the news about Grace—or even *what* to tell him.

She turned around. Someone was rowing toward them, but she couldn't tell if it was Caleb. The person's silhouette was covered in darkness from the tall trees on both sides of the river.

She squinted. Whoever it was, was moving quickly. The closer the boat came, she could make out the dark hair and dark eyes. She frowned. It definitely wasn't her twin brother, who had hair as blond as hers.

She dropped the worm. The man rowing toward them was wearing a leather jacket and tattered blue jeans.

Ethan. What is he doing here?

A minute later, he rowed up beside their boat, coming to a stop. He positioned his boat so he was parallel to where she sat and tied his boat to hers.

He picked up a bouquet of lilacs in his lap and handed them to her. "These are for you."

"I don't want them." She pursed her lips. "Why are you here?"

His Adam's apple bobbed up and down. "To fight for you."

"What are you talking about?"

Ethan stood and stepped into their boat. The boat shook from side to side as he sat down across from her. As he spoke, he twisted the bouquet in his hands. "I came back to see you as soon as I arrived. But when I came to your house, Tyler was proposing to you. I saw the two of you hugging."

So that was why Ethan hadn't spoken to her. He thought she was engaged. "Ethan, I—"

"When I was in Greece, all I could think about was

you. I couldn't stand being so far apart from you, so I came back." Setting the flowers on his lap, he leaned forward and reached for her hands. "From the moment we met, we were all wrong for one another."

She bit her bottom lip. Where was he going with this?

"The more I've thought about it, though ..." Ethan entwined their fingers, his thumbs caressing the inside of her palms. "I think we met at just the right time, at just the right place, to be perfectly right together."

His words left her breathless, thinking back to their conversation on the River Boat Cruise. Ethan thought they were perfect together. She wasn't just a fling. He hadn't just spent time with her because he'd made a deal with Dad.

Her heart beat faster. But they still had his family to consider. "What about your parents?"

"I told them about you. They aren't too happy, but they aren't stopping me either. In fact, my mom is the one who encouraged me to come tonight."

"But you only have a few weeks left in the US. It's not like this can go anywhere."

He quirked an eyebrow and smiled. "As soon as I'm done training my colleagues, I'll come back and apply for a green card. And I'll do it if ..." He broke the space between them, their faces inches apart. "... if you choose me instead of Tyler."

Amanda lifted her left hand and wiggled her ringless finger. "I didn't say yes. I couldn't."

"Why not?" Ethan asked.

"Because my heart was given to someone else."

Ethan's smile widened, deepening the cleft in his chin. He ran a hand down her cheek. "Me?"

Nodding, she inched forward and wrapped her arms around his neck. "I'm sorry I asked you to leave the hospital room. I shouldn't have blamed you. It wasn't your fault. In fact, I'm so grateful for the care my dad received from you and the other doctors at Furnam Hospital. He's still alive because of you."

"He's alive because of you too. All of your good choices regarding his health—you made his immune system strong enough to fight off the infection." Ethan put his hands on her lower back. "We make a good team, don't we?"

"The best."

"I want you to know, you changed my mind. I do want to get married and start a family one day." Ethan rested his forehead against hers. "I love you, Amanda."

"I love you, too, Ethan." She grinned. "What would you say if my dad and I stayed in Greece while you're there? My dad can finish his treatment with you as his doctor, and I'd love to get out of here for a while. Wouldn't you, Dad?"

On the other side of the boat, Dad whistled. "Who-ee! As long as I get to fish every day!"

Ethan laughed. "Of course you can, Ray."

"You really think we're all wrong for each other, huh?" she asked.

"Please tell me that's not the only thing you remember from what I said."

Amanda giggled mischievously. "Oh, yes. You also think we're perfect together." She brought her lips to his, igniting a fire that burned deep within her core.

She kissed him soft and slow, savoring this moment. Her chest burst with pure joy. Over the last several months, life had turned upside down, yet somehow it had turned out better than she'd ever expected.

Author's Note

Dear Reader,

Creating depth and complexity for Amanda and Ethan made me want to yank my hair out. I couldn't get them right. Part of my problem was that I hadn't spent much time in a hospital. But before I wrote my final draft, my youngest daughter was born with congenital lobar emphysema (the same condition as Mac and Charlie's baby). I spent weeks at the hospital as doctors and nurses tried to figure out why my daughter couldn't breathe on her own. Once doctors diagnosed her, they immediately performed surgery, and successfully removed part of her lung.

Several months after my daughter came home from the hospital, I started revising the final draft of *Shattered Heart.* In that final revision, I breathed my life experiences into Amanda and Ethan, and poured my heart and soul into their deepest struggles.

I hope you enjoyed their love story, and I hope you enjoyed your time in Maple Valley once again.

XOXO,
Crystal

P.S. My daughter is now thriving and growing like her older siblings.

P.P.S. If you have a minute, please consider leaving a review. Book reviews help other readers discover which books are right for them. Thank you in advance for leaving your opinion. It matters so much to me!

Acknowledgments

I'm an extrovert. The hardest part about being a writer is the quiet alone time. I love being around people and sharing experiences with others. The more the merrier, in my opinion. This is why *Shattered Heart* has been such a fun book to write. So many people have offered their time, knowledge, and expertise to make *Shattered Heart* more realistic and more meaningful than I ever dreamed. This novel would not be the same without the following teams …

My family—My favorite team of all! Mike, Landon, Zoey, Savannah, Mom, Dad, Julie, David, Lisa, and Ben, your support means the world to me. I could not do this without you!

My dear friends—Jen, Mandie, Carly, Jenny, Lyra, and Sarah, I feel blessed to have you as friends, and I appreciate your constant support in everything I do.

My book team—Janice, Lauren, Lyndsey, and Lisa, I love the changes and edits you suggested, I love my cover, and I love my bookmarks. Oh, and I love, love, love that you are all a part of *Shattered Heart's* creation.

My beta readers—Oh my goodness! I can't believe how many of you offered to read one of the initial drafts of *Shattered Heart*. Each of you offered such insightful feedback!

My research team—Dr. Gall, Carly, Alyssa, Jamie, Jenna, Stan, Jodi, Suzanne, and Nicole—What would I have done without you? You taught me so much about cancer treatment, hospitals, labor/delivery, and the emotional turmoil of experiencing a life-threatening disease. Nicole, thank you for answering all of my texts and questions when I first started writing this book. I thought you'd be here to read the final copy. I hope you knew how grateful I was for your help. Rest in peace.

My writing group, the Quad City Scribblers—I get goosebumps thinking about how our relationships have blossomed over the years and how far each of our journeys have come. I look forward to seeing what the future will bring for you.

My reader team, Crystal's Crew—I've had a blast brainstorming with you and sharing updates. You guys rock!

My readers—You are the reason I write. I thoroughly enjoyed creating Amanda and Ethan's love story for you!

God—Thank you for bringing all of these people into my life.

Reader's Guide

1. At the beginning of the novel, Amanda breaks up with Tyler. Would you have reacted similarly to her? Why or why not?
2. Amanda and Ethan disagree about healthcare. Do you prefer holistic practices, traditional healthcare, or does it depend on the medical issue?
3. Amanda finds it difficult to support her dad's decision to do chemotherapy. Why is it so hard for her?
4. Ray meddles with Amanda and Ethan's love life. Do you have anyone who meddles in your life? Do you find it endearing or annoying?
5. Ethan decided to keep his ex-wife's fraud a secret. What does his choice say about him?
6. Ray tells Amanda: "Sometimes people have secrets to protect those they love." Do secrets protect others or hurt them? Or does it depend on the secret?
7. Why was Grace hesitant to divulge the truth about her past? Would you have reacted similarly?

8. Ethan struggles to keep his relationship with Amanda platonic. What draws him to Amanda?
9. Amanda can't wait to get married and start a family. Does her mindset change throughout the novel?
10. What is your favorite moment between Amanda and Ethan?

About the Author

Crystal Joy lives in Iowa with her husband and three growing children. She's a stay-at-home mom with a heart for people. She loves getting to know them, writing about them, and inventing them. When she's not hanging out with the hero and heroine in her latest book, she loves to dance awkwardly, watch reality TV, and visit real locations from her favorite books.

You can learn more about Crystal Joy at her website www.crystaljoybooks.com.